C L A S S I C
F A I R Y
T A L E S

PUBLICATIONS INTERNATIONAL, LTD.

Cover illustrated by Phil Wilson

Title page illustrated by Sherry Neidigh

Louis Weber, C.E.O.
Publications International, Ltd.
7373 North Cicero Avenue
Lincolnwood, Illinois 60646

Once upon a time...

CONTENTS

Cinderella

Adapted by Jane Jerrard
Illustrated by Susan Spellman

Once upon a time, there was a young girl, as sweet as sugar, as kind as a mother's kiss, and as pretty as the sun setting in the sky.

The girl had a very mean stepmother who made her life miserable. The stepmother and her two nasty daughters treated the girl as a servant. They always made her scrub the floors and wash the dishes and pick up after them. They called the girl Cinderella because at day's end she would sit among the cinders on the hearth and warm her tired bones.

Cinderella was always cheerful and polite. Her kindness made her beautiful, and her beauty shone like sunlight through the dirt on her face and her ragged clothing.

Cinderella's stepmother and stepsisters spent their days preening in front of a mirror and talking about which one of them would marry the handsome prince of the kingdom. Cinderella was always too busy mending their dresses and fixing their hair to think about the prince.

One day something very exciting arrived. It was an invitation to the prince's fancy ball! All the fine people in the land were invited, and the sisters worried about what to wear and how to behave with royalty. In preparation for the ball, they began to treat Cinderella even more cruelly than before.

Cinderella sewed and ironed for days, but the poor girl was not allowed to go to the ball herself. She was only a servant. Besides, she did not have a dress nice enough for the ball.

Finally the night arrived. As Cinderella helped her younger stepsister into her gown, the cruel girl asked, "Cinderella, why don't you come with us to the ball and dance with the prince?"

The stepmother and her daughters laughed at the thought of dirty, barefoot Cinderella dancing with the handsome prince. Saddened, Cinderella looked down at the floor.

As the stepmother and her daughters climbed into their coach and rode off to the ball, Cinderella began to cry. Cinderella never complained, but the day of the fancy ball was too disappointing for her to bear.

"Why must I stay at home and sweep up the hearth while everyone else goes to the ball? Am I not as good and kind as everyone else?" cried Cinderella. She wanted to put on a fine dress. She wanted to dance in the palace hall. Most of all she wanted to catch a glimpse of the handsome prince. Maybe he would ask her to dance with him!

Suddenly a beautiful fairy magically appeared. It was Cinderella's fairy godmother!

"What is wrong, dear Cinderella?" asked the fairy godmother. Even though she had secretly watched over Cinderella's hard life, this was the first time she had ever seen the girl cry.

Cinderella explained that she wanted very much to go to the ball to meet the prince.

"And so you shall go, Cinderella, for you have always, always been good," said her fairy godmother.

Cinderella could not believe her ears.

"But I have no coach to take me there," she said.

"Not to worry, my dear," replied Cinderella's fairy godmother. With her special magic, she turned a hollow pumpkin into a handsome coach decorated with gold and velvet. Cinderella could not believe her eyes.

"But who will drive the coach?" she asked.

Cinderella's fairy godmother found six mice, and waving her wand over them, turned them into six fine, gray horses, ready to pull Cinderella's carriage. All that was missing was a driver. A fat, white rat was just the thing!

"Now, sweet girl, you can go to the ball!" said the fairy godmother.

"But my clothes. . . ," whispered Cinderella. "I cannot go to the fancy ball in dirty rags!"

With one touch of her sparkling wand, her fairy godmother turned Cinderella's old dress into a lovely silk gown trimmed in gold. Best of all she gave the girl a pair of tiny glass slippers that fit just right!

"Oh, thank you, fairy godmother!" cried Cinderella. "This will be the most wonderful night of my life!"

With the help of her handsome footman, Cinderella stepped into the magical pumpkin coach. A shiver of excitement ran through her. Was this a dream? She pinched herself and decided that it was not.

Just as the carriage was about to pull away, Cinderella's fairy godmother called to her.

"You must be home before midnight, Cinderella," she warned, "because my magic will disappear when the clock strikes twelve o'clock!"

"I won't be late, fairy godmother. Thank you!" Cinderella waved out the window of her coach, pretending to be a real princess.

Off she rode to the ball. The whole way there, her heart pounded with anticipation. When the carriage arrived at the palace, Cinderella looked out to see a great gold clock at the top of one of the towers.

"Good," she sighed. "Now I can be sure that I won't be late."

Cinderella stepped out of her coach and gracefully climbed the stairs to the palace. When she appeared in the doorway of the ballroom, everyone at the ball turned to look at her. Cinderella was far more beautiful than any of the princesses, duchesses, and noble ladies in attendance. The other guests hushed as Cinderella walked down the staircase.

The prince was busy greeting his guests when he looked up to see Cinderella. He took one look at her and fell in love with the beautiful girl. In fact everyone at the ball fell in love with her. Aside from being lovely, Cinderella was also charming and sweet. As the prince and Cinderella danced, all the people smiled and watched. No one recognized her, not even her stepsisters and stepmother.

The prince asked Cinderella to dance every dance. Cinderella discovered that aside from being a very handsome prince, he was also very kind. Cinderella was so happy she forgot the time. The clock sounded the ninth stroke of the midnight hour when Cinderella remembered the promise she had made to her fairy godmother.

On the tenth stroke, Cinderella dashed out of the ballroom without another word to the prince, leaving him and the rest of the guests astonished!

On the eleventh stroke, she flew down the palace steps in such a hurry that she left one of her glass slippers behind.

On the twelfth stroke, Cinderella's dress was transformed back into tattered rags. She ran as fast as she could from the palace so that no one would recognize her.

The prince ran after Cinderella, but it was too late. She was already gone. He wanted to call out to her, but he realized that she had never told him her name! The prince spied the glass slipper on the palace steps. It must belong to her, he thought. He vowed to to find the slipper's mysterious owner.

Cinderella ran all the way home, dressed in her rags. Her coach had turned back into a pumpkin, and the mice and the rat had all run away. All she had left of her beautiful evening at the ball was the other glass slipper.

The next day everyone in the land could talk of nothing but the ball and the beautiful stranger who had stolen the prince's heart.

The prince was determined to find the girl he loved. "This tiny glass slipper is all that I have," he thought. "I must use it to try to find her." That very day he began to search over all the land, trying to find the maiden who could wear the delicate glass slipper.

At last the young prince arrived at the house where Cinderella lived. The stepsisters both tried to fit their large feet into the slipper. It was plain to see that neither of these ladies was the mysterious stranger from the ball.

Cinderella had been watching from beside the fire. She asked softly, "May I please try?" Her stepmother and stepsisters laughed and told her not to waste the prince's precious time.

The prince knelt and held out the glass slipper for Cinderella. Her foot slipped into it with ease! Cinderella pulled the other glass slipper from her apron pocket and put it on, too.

"It fits!" shrieked the stepmother.

"It fits!" howled the stepsisters.

"It fits!" sang Cinderella's fairy godmother, waving her wand and dressing Cinderella in a beautiful gown.

Cinderella went back to the palace with the prince. He was so overcome with love and joy that he married her that very day!

Hansel and Gretel

Adapted by Sarah Toast
Illustrated by Susan Spellman

Long ago a poor woodcutter lived with his family on the outskirts of a large forest. He had two children named Hansel and Gretel. The children's loving mother had died, and the stepmother did not like children.

When hard times came and even the rich had very little, the woodcutter's family had nothing at all. At last the woodcutter said, "How can we feed our poor children when there isn't even enough for ourselves?"

His wife answered, "We must take the children into the woods and leave them there to take care of themselves. That way maybe we all will have a chance. Otherwise, all four of us will starve."

Hansel heard what his stepmother had said. When he told Gretel what their parents had planned, she began to cry. "But we are only children. How can we manage in the woods with no one to take care of us?" she wept.

"Hush, Gretel," said Hansel. "We'll think of something." Hansel was older than his sister. He knew he would have to think of a way to take care of them both.

That night Hansel waited until his parents were asleep and the house was quiet. Then he tiptoed carefully out of the house and down to the gravel road. He filled the pockets of his trousers and coat with small white stones, then crept back into the house and went to bed.

The next morning the parents woke the children early. "You have to come with us deep into the forest to gather wood," their father explained, looking sadly at the children. "We have no money to buy firewood in the village." The stepmother handed them each a small piece of bread to nibble on, and off they went. Hansel lagged behind the rest of the family, dropping stones on the ground from time to time.

By the time the family was deep in the forest, the children and their parents had all collected as much wood as they could carry. The woodcutter told the children that he and their stepmother needed to chop the wood into small logs that would be easier to carry home.

"But you children must be tired from our long walk," he said to them. "I will build you a fire so that you can take a nap while we go and cut the wood." He kissed both Hansel and Gretel and set to work building them a fire.

Soon the children's faces glowed in the light of a warm fire. "Eat your bread and then lie down by the fire," said the stepmother. "We will be back soon, after we have cut the wood."

The children were so tired that they could not even finish their bread, but fell fast asleep right away in front of the cozy fire. When they awoke, they were alone in the dark woods.

"How will we ever get out of this forest?" cried Gretel. But Hansel told her that when the moon came up, they would find their way home. Sure enough, when the bright moon rose, they could see the white stones that pointed toward home.

The tired children reached their cottage at daybreak. Their father was very happy to see them. He had never wanted to leave them in the woods. He had also sold the firewood for a good price, so for a while there was enough to eat.

The stepmother was not happy to see the children. "Why did you allow them to come home?" she angrily asked her husband. "We will run out of food. You will see."

Sadly, the stepmother was right. Hard times soon came again. Early one morning the parents led the children back into the woods. Hansel didn't have time to collect white stones to help them find their way home. All he had was a crust of stale bread. At first Hansel worried that he and Gretel would be lost, but then he had an idea.

"Don't worry," he later told Gretel after their parents had left them in the woods. "I made a trail of breadcrumbs so we can find our way back home."

Hansel and Gretel slept until the moon rose and then set out to find the trail. But, alas, the hungry birds of the forest had eaten every crumb. The poor children were truly lost.

Hansel and Gretel walked all night and all the next day. On the morning of the third day, they were almost too weak to walk another step.

"We will never find our way out of the woods," cried Gretel. "And I am too hungry to walk any farther." Just when she was ready to give up, Gretel looked up and saw a beautiful white bird sitting on a branch above her. The bird sang to the children, and then it flew on ahead. The bird was so pretty that for a moment Gretel forgot how hungry and tired she was.

The children followed the white bird to a clearing in the woods, where they saw a beautiful house made of gingerbread and candy. Its doorway was made of butterscotch and its shutters were made of icing. The hungry children broke off pieces of the house and began to eat. Their mouths were full of candy when they heard a sweet and gentle voice:

Nibble, nibble, like a mouse.

Who is nibbling on my house?

The door opened and an old, old woman hobbled out. She came along slowly because she couldn't see very well.

At first the children were very frightened of the strange old woman. But they quickly changed their minds when she reached out to them with her wrinkled hands and said kindly, "You poor, hungry children. You must be starving! But you do not have to eat pieces of my old house. Come inside and I will give you much better food than this."

The old woman gave Hansel and Gretel a very large meal of pancakes, apples, and milk. They had never before seen so much food on one table! Hansel and Gretel ate hungrily and happily. Then the kind old woman put them to sleep in soft beds with warm covers.

As Hansel and Gretel slept soundly, their bellies full with all sorts of delicious sweets from the old woman's gingerbread house, the old woman prepared more food for them.

All through the night, she made apple dumplings, cakes, and pies for the two poor children. As she baked these treats, the old woman grinned and hummed to herself. When she peeked in the bedroom to check on the sleeping children, the old woman chuckled out loud.

Hansel and Gretel stayed with the old woman for many days, all the while eating her delicious food. Hansel and Gretel never guessed that the woman, who seemed so nice, was truly very wicked. She had built her house of cakes and candies just to attract children so she could eat them!

Soon Hansel and Gretel began to grow a little bit plump. The old woman noticed this and began to get hungry herself. Early one morning before the sun had completely risen, she dragged Hansel out of his warm bed. She locked him inside a wooden cage. Then she woke Gretel.

"Fetch some water and some dumplings for your brother," she told the girl. "Fatten him up for me to eat!"

Gretel began to cry. The wicked old woman ignored Gretel's tears and made her cook and clean all day long.

Every morning the old woman told Hansel to hold out his finger so she could feel how fat he was growing. But Hansel knew that the old woman could not see well, so he held out an old bone for her to feel. This clever trick made her believe that Hansel was still too thin to eat.

After four weeks Hansel still didn't seem any fatter to the old woman. But she was very hungry by this time. She decided to eat him anyway and Gretel as well.

The old woman heated up her great big oven and then called Gretel into the kitchen. She told the girl to climb into the big oven to see if it was hot enough to bake bread. But Gretel knew exactly what the old woman was planning. She knew better than to get into the oven, and told the old woman she didn't know how to open the heavy oven door.

"Foolish little girl," said the wicked old woman. She pulled open the oven door.

"But I don't know how to crawl inside," said Gretel, pretending to be confused.

The old woman sighed impatiently. "Foolish, foolish little girl!" she grumbled. She leaned into the oven to show Gretel how to fit inside. Gretel was a smart little girl and she knew just what to do. She gave the old woman a big shove that sent her tumbling all the way in. Then Gretel banged the door shut. She ran to free Hansel.

"Hansel, we're saved! The mean old woman is dead!" cried Gretel. She unlocked Hansel's cage, and they hugged each other and danced around the room.

Then the two children found the old woman's treasure of gold and jewels. When they left, they stuffed the gold in a sack and filled their pockets with jewels.

After hours of walking, Hansel and Gretel came to a lake. Gretel called to a white swan, who agreed to take the children across. On the other side Hansel and Gretel found the path for home. When they saw their own house and their father, they ran to him.

The woodcutter laughed and cried with joy to see his children again. He had been very sad since his evil wife had made him leave them in the forest. The stepmother had died while the children were gone. Since her death the woodcutter had been searching the woods for his children day and night.

The woodcutter threw his arms around the children. Excitedly, they showed him the gold and jewels. Their worries were over, and the family lived happily.

The Three Little Pigs

Adapted by Jane Jerrard
Illustrated by Susan Spellman

One day mother pig told her three little pigs that it was time for them to go out into the world to make their own way. Each little pig decided to go and build himself a little house.

The first little pig met a man with a bundle of straw. "This straw will make a fine house," said the little pig proudly. He bought all the man's straw and built a fine little house.

Soon a mean and hungry wolf came upon the little straw house. The wolf knocked on the door and said, "Little pig! Little pig! Let me come in!"

"Not by the hair on my chinny chin chin!" squealed the pig.

"Then I'll huff, and I'll puff, and I'll blow your house in!" said the wolf.

The wolf huffed, and he puffed, and he blew the house in. He blew so hard that he blew the little pig away.

The second little pig met a man with a great bundle of sticks for sale. "These sticks will make a fine house," said the second little pig. He bought the sticks from the man and built his house with them. It was a much stronger house than his brother's straw house had been.

It wasn't long before the wolf came along to the little stick house. He knocked on the door, saying, "Little pig! Little pig! Let me come in!"

The little pig peeked out his window and saw the wolf on his doorstep. "Not by the hair on my chinny chin chin!" he squealed nervously.

"Then I'll huff, and I'll puff, and I'll blow your house in!" threatened the wolf.

The wolf huffed, and he puffed, and he blew the house in. He blew so hard that he blew away the second little pig, too.

The third little pig was a very smart pig. He thought for a long time about what kind of house he would like to have. One day he met a man who had a load of bricks for sale. "These bricks will make a fine and sturdy house," said the little pig confidently.

Then the third little pig bought all the man's bricks and built himself a handsome little house. It was stronger than his first brother's house of straw, and sturdier than his second brother's house of sticks.

Soon after the brick house was finished, the mean and hungry wolf came pounding on the door. "Little pig! Little pig! Let me come in!"

"Not by the hair on my chinny chin chin!" squealed the third little pig. He stood his ground inside his front door.

"Then I'll huff, and I'll puff, and I'll blow your house in!" roared the wolf.

The wolf huffed, and he puffed, and he huffed and puffed some more, but he could not blow the little pig's house in.

"Silly old wolf! He will never blow my house in!" the third little pig squealed and giggled inside his sturdy house.

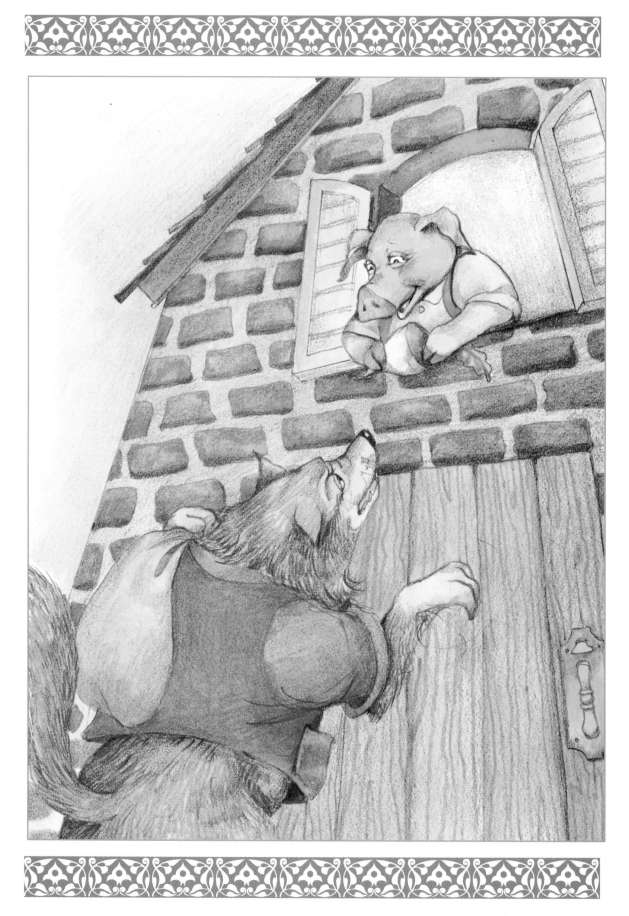

The wolf heard the little pig laughing at him and began to get angry. He was a very proud wolf, and he did not like to be laughed at. The wolf made up his mind to have the third little pig for dinner one night. He thought up a plan. "Little pig," he said, "I know where there is a nice field of turnips."

This caught the little pig's attention. Turnips were his favorite thing to eat. "Where is this field of turnips?" the little pig asked the wolf, poking his head out the window.

"At Farmer Brown's," he said. "I'll take you there at six o'clock tomorrow morning." The wolf licked his chops and thought about the fine pig dinner he would have the next day.

The little pig agreed to meet the wolf. But pigs are much smarter than wolves, and he knew this wolf was up to no good. The little pig got up at five o'clock the next morning and went to Farmer Brown's all by himself. He got the turnips and was back in his house when the wolf arrived at six.

"Little pig, are you ready?" he asked.

"Ready!" scoffed the pig. "I've already gone and come back with lots of turnips!"

The wolf was very angry that he had been tricked, so he tried to trick the pig again.

"Little pig," he said sweetly, "I know where there is a tree full of juicy apples."

The little pig loved apples almost as much as turnips. "Where is this apple tree?" asked the pig.

"In Granny Smith's garden," said the wolf. "I'll come for you tomorrow at five o'clock in the morning. We will go together."

The little pig woke at four o'clock and went off to find the apples. The wolf also got up at four o'clock, but the pig was not home. The wolf went to the apple tree.

The little pig was just about to come down from the tree with some apples when he saw the wolf below.

The little pig was very frightened. The wolf came close and called up to him.

"My, you're up early," said the wolf. "How are the apples?"

The pig thought quickly. "Delicious!" he said. "Why don't you stand back, and I will throw one down to you."

The wolf took a few steps back.

The little pig tossed the apple as far as he could. He threw the apple so far that the wolf had to run after it to catch it. The wolf ran so far that the little pig was able to collect a whole armload of apples before he scooted down the tree and ran away. "Silly old wolf," the little pig squealed and giggled. He was safe at home before the wolf found the apple he had thrown.

The little pig brought all of the apples into his kitchen. "I think I will invite my brothers to have dinner at my new house," he said. He made apple fritters and applesauce and apple pie, and he still had plenty of apples left to eat for a snack.

When the third little pig's brothers came to dinner that night, they admired his fine brick house. "This is much sturdier than a straw house," moped the first little pig.

"And much stronger than a stick house," added the second little pig glumly.

In the meantime the wolf was furious that he had been tricked again. He thought he was trickier than any little pig, and this little pig had tricked him too many times already. So he thought and he thought until he came up with another plan.

The next morning the wolf went over to the little pig's house. He knocked on the door and said in his friendliest voice, "Little pig, there is a fair in town today. There are so many wonderful things to do there. Let's go together! I'll come by for you at three this afternoon."

The little pig agreed, but he did not wait for the wolf. The clever pig started out early for the fair. He tasted pies at the pie booth and smelled flowers at the flower booth. He even had a tall glass of lemonade at the lemonade booth. He rode around and around on the carousel and way up high on the ferris wheel.

"What a wonderful day at the fair!" the little pig said happily. "But I think it's time for me to go home." The little pig wanted to get back to his sturdy brick house before the wolf showed up at the fair.

On his way out of the fair, the little pig bought a great big barrel so he would have a place to store his apples and turnips. The little pig was on his way home with his barrel when he saw the wolf coming up the hill towards him.

"Oh dear, here comes that pesky wolf," fretted the little pig.

The little pig had to hide from the wolf. He knew that the wolf wanted to eat him for dinner. "I know just what to do!" he said to himself. The tricky little pig crawled into the barrel. But in a moment the barrel started to roll down the hill with the little pig in it.

The barrel rolled over and over, gaining speed on its way down the hill. The wolf looked up to see the barrel headed straight for him. This strange sight frightened the wolf so much that he ran right home. He forgot all about meeting the little pig and never went to the fair at all.

The little pig rolled all the way home inside the barrel. He was very dizzy when he finally crawled out. "At least I got away from that nasty old wolf," he said, dusting himself off.

The wolf went to the little pig's house the next day. "Little pig," he said, "I was going to meet you at the fair yesterday, when all at once the most frightening thing came rolling down the hill. I ran straight home!"

The little pig laughed. "Ha, ha! It was I that frightened you! I was in the barrel!"

The wolf was very angry when he heard the little pig say this. He made up his mind then and there to eat the little pig for dinner that very day. The wolf's mouth began to water as he looked at the pig.

"Little pig," roared the wolf, "I am going to eat you for dinner today! I may not have been able to blow your house in, and I may not have been able to trick you, but I'm going to come down the chimney to get you now!"

With that the wolf leaped onto the roof. "Here I come, little pig!" he snarled down into the chimney.

But it happened that the little pig was having his brothers over for dinner again that night. He had hung a pot full of boiling water over the fire so that he could make a fine stew. The wolf tumbled down the chimney right into the big pot of boiling water. The pig quickly put a heavy lid on the pot, and that was the end of the wolf.

That night the little pig invited both of his brothers to live with him in his sturdy brick house. All three little pigs lived happily ever after.

Snow White

Adapted by Jane Jerrard
Illustrated by Burgandy Nilles

L ong ago in a far-off land, a princess was born with hair as black as night, skin as white as snow, and lips the color of rubies. She was called Snow White.

As the baby grew into a little girl, she became more beautiful every year. Her stepmother, the queen, was also very beautiful. The queen was so vain she had a magical mirror made. Every day she looked in the mirror and asked,

> *Mirror, mirror on the wall,*
>
> *Who is fairest of us all?*

The mirror would answer,

> *You, my queen, are fairest in the land.*

And the queen was very pleased, because she knew that it was true.

Every day the mirror told the vain queen that there was no one fairer than she. But the queen never grew more beautiful from one day to the next. Snow White, on the other hand, was becoming lovelier with each passing day.

One day, when Snow White had grown to be a young maiden, the vain queen asked,

> *Mirror, mirror on the wall,*
>
> *Who is fairest of us all?*

And the mirror replied,

> *You, my queen, may lovely be,*
>
> *But Snow White is fairer still than thee.*

The queen was very angry. She could not stand to have anyone be prettier than she. From that time on, the queen hated Snow White. When she could no longer bear to look at the beautiful princess, she called a woodsman and ordered him to take Snow White away and kill her.

The man, fearing for his own life, took the girl deep into the forest but could not bring himself to carry out the order. Instead he left Snow White there alone.

The woodsman returned to the evil queen and told her that Snow White had escaped from him in the woods. The queen was very angry that Snow White was still alive. She banished the woodsman from the kingdom forever.

Snow White had never been all by herself in the woods before. Around her were mysterious noises and frightening shadows. She was so scared, she began to run. Tree branches caught at her black hair as she ran through the forest. Wild beasts watched her, but they did not harm the beautiful girl.

Snow White ran as fast and as far as she could, until she came to a little clearing among the trees. There she saw a small cottage with a red roof.

"Maybe someone here will be able to help me," sighed Snow White with relief. She knocked and knocked on the front door. When no one answered, Snow White went inside.

There she found a tiny little table set with seven plates. "What a cute little table!" she exclaimed. Snow White was very hungry after her long day in the woods, and so she nibbled a few bites of food from each of the little plates.

After her snack, Snow White explored the rest of the cottage. She found a little bedroom with seven tiny beds. Suddenly Snow White realized she was very sleepy.

"I hope they don't mind if I take a little nap," she yawned, crawling under the covers of the seventh little bed. Soon she was fast asleep.

The cottage Snow White had discovered belonged to seven dwarfs. Soon after Snow White fell asleep, the dwarfs came back from the gold and copper mines where they worked. They all sat down at the table and quickly discovered that someone had been nibbling at their food.

Soon they made an even greater discovery—a beautiful young maiden asleep in their bedroom. Because Snow White looked so peaceful, they let her sleep until morning.

When Snow White awoke, she was delighted to meet her seven new friends. She told them all about the evil queen and her adventure in the woods. The seven dwarfs felt sorry for Snow White and asked her to stay. She took care of the cottage, and the dwarfs gave her food, friendship, and shelter in return.

Snow White was happy living with the dwarfs. She came to love them all so much that she forgot about the evil queen who was so jealous of her beauty.

The evil queen thought that Snow White had perished in the woods. But one day she went to her mirror and again asked,

> *Mirror, mirror on the wall,*
>
> *Who is fairest of us all?*

The mirror replied,

> *You, my queen, may lovely be,*
>
> *But Snow White is fairer still than thee.*

Then the queen knew that Snow White was still alive. She decided to kill the girl herself. The queen disguised herself as an ugly old woman and searched the woods for Snow White. One day she appeared at the dwarfs' cottage. She called out, "Belts for sale! Buy my pretty belts!"

Snow White saw no danger in opening the door to a poor, ugly old woman. Snow White tried on one of the lovely silk belts. The queen pulled the belt so tight around the girl's waist that she fell down as if she were dead.

The queen threw off her old woman's costume and shouted, "I will *always* be the fairest of all!" With that, she left Snow White lying on the floor and returned to her castle.

When the dwarfs returned from the mines that day, they found Snow White lying in their house. "Our dear Snow White!" they cried. Right away they saw that the girl's belt was too tight and cut it off with a knife. She began to breathe again and told them what had happened.

The dwarfs realized that the old woman must have been the evil queen, and they warned Snow White to be very careful.

"Above all," said the oldest dwarf, "you must never, never open the door for anyone." Snow White promised to obey.

Meanwhile, when the queen arrived back at her castle, she asked once more,

> *Mirror, mirror on the wall,*
>
> *Who is fairest of us all?*

When the mirror answered that Snow White was still the fairest, the queen shook with rage and vowed that Snow White must die.

The evil queen set out for the cottage in a new disguise. This time she knocked at the window of the cottage. Recalling the dwarfs' stern warning about the door, Snow White thought it safe to open the window.

The old woman offered to sell Snow White a lovely comb. Snow White took the comb through the window and put it in her hair. She sank to the ground right where she stood. The comb was poisoned.

The dwarfs soon came home. They realized at once what had happened and quickly removed the comb from Snow White's hair. Then the dwarfs warned her again.

"Snow White, you must never, never open the door or the window for anyone!" said the littlest dwarf, shaking his finger at her.

Back at the castle the queen asked yet again,

> *Mirror, mirror on the wall,*
>
> *Who is fairest of us all?*

The mirror replied,

> *Lovely, my queen, indeed you are,*
>
> *But Snow White is still lovelier by far!*

When the evil queen learned that the princess still lived, she was furious. "I must find a way to be rid of Snow White forever!" she cried.

The queen used all her evil magic to make a single perfect, poisoned apple. Then the queen dressed herself as a poor woman and went once more to see Snow White.

This time Snow White was busy planting flowers in the garden. The dwarfs had warned her not to open the door or window for strangers, but they had never said anything about talking to strangers outside.

The queen offered the girl the apple, and it looked so delicious that Snow White could not resist it. Part of the apple's magic was that everyone who saw it must taste it. Snow White bit into the fruit. She instantly fell down as if dead.

When the queen returned to the castle, her mirror told her at last, "Queen, thou art fairest of us all!"

The dwarfs could not wake Snow White, but she looked as healthy and as pretty as if she were comfortably sleeping. They laid her in a glass case so they could watch over her.

Day and night the dwarfs took turns watching over Snow White. One day a prince was hunting in the woods. He came upon Snow White lying in the glass case and asked the dwarf on guard who she was.

"She is our dear Snow White, put to sleep by the spell of an evil queen," replied the dwarf sadly.

The prince gazed into the glass case. "This is the most beautiful princess I have ever seen." he said, gazing at Snow White's black hair, white skin, and ruby-red lips. Instantly the prince fell deeply in love.

The prince opened the case and lifted Snow White in his arms. As the prince picked up Snow White, the piece of poisoned apple fell from her mouth, and she awoke. Snow White slowly opened her eyes to find herself in the arms of the prince!

When the dwarfs learned that Snow White was alive, they danced with joy and agreed happily that she should marry the handsome prince.

As for the queen, her hatred made her so ugly that she could no longer bear to look in her mirror.

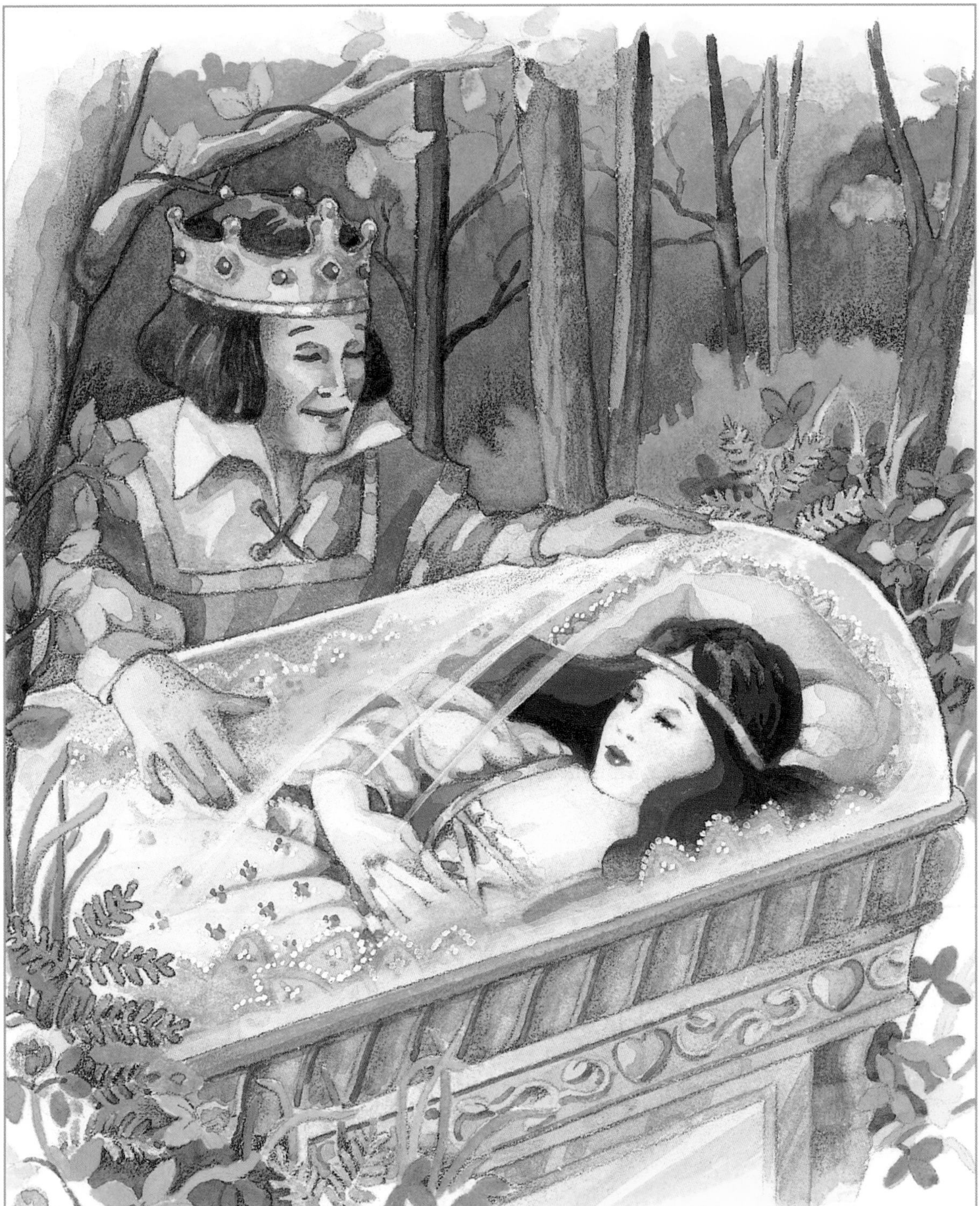

The Velveteen Rabbit

Adapted by Jennifer Boudart
Illustrated by Elena Kucharik

On Christmas morning the boy couldn't wait to go downstairs and see what Santa had brought him. Normally the boy's stocking was filled with candy, but this year it held a wonderful surprise: a velveteen rabbit.

The boy was filled with joy when he saw the velveteen rabbit. He kissed the rabbit and squeezed its soft, squishy tummy. The boy held his new friend under his arm while he opened all of his other gifts. That Christmas the boy received many new toys which joined his old toys in the nursery. With so many toys, the boy forgot about the velveteen rabbit for a time. But the velveteen rabbit did not forget how nice it felt to be held in the boy's arms.

The nursery was filled with many different sorts of toys. There was a shiny toy soldier who looked very serious and dignified, a bright sailboat that really floated, and a bright green car that buzzed and moved.

The velveteen rabbit felt very plain next to these toys. He was nothing but fluff and stitches. The only toy in the nursery who became friends with the velveteen rabbit was a shabby old horse. The horse had been played with so many times, that his ear was held on with a pin. Although he was old and frayed, the horse was very wise. "Flashy toys don't last," said the horse. "They break too easily, and they don't have anything lovable inside. They will never be real."

"What does it mean to be real?" asked the velveteen rabbit. "Does it mean being new forever?"

"No," explained the horse. "You become real after someone loves you for a long time. By then you are old and tattered, but that's okay. When you are real, you are truly beautiful!"

This impressed the velveteen rabbit. He wanted to be real!

That night when the boy was about to go to bed he asked the nanny, "Will you find my toy dog, please? It's the one I always hold at night."

The nanny was not in the mood to look for the toy dog. She glanced at the nursery floor and picked up the velveteen rabbit. She handed it to the boy's outstretched arms. "Here you go," she said. "He'll help you get to sleep just fine."

The boy took the velveteen rabbit and held him tightly next to his body. The velveteen rabbit fit the crook of the boy's arm much better than the toy dog did, and the boy quickly and happily fell fast asleep.

The velveteen rabbit felt so good that he didn't mind being a bit squashed. In fact, he didn't even notice. The velveteen rabbit loved being hugged so closely while the boy slept. Of all the toys in the nursery, the velveteen rabbit felt like he was the most special.

That night the boy dreamed he was the captain of a great ship. He sailed the ship with the velveteen rabbit at his side.

From that night on, the velveteen rabbit always looked forward to bedtime. The boy would hug him as he fell asleep. In the boy's dreams, he and the velveteen rabbit had more wonderful adventures.

The boy also spent the day with the velveteen rabbit. The boy loved the velveteen rabbit so much that he took him everywhere he went. Sometimes they went on picnics or played in the garden. Once the velveteen rabbit watched as the boy helped his mother plant carrots. Another time the boy treated the velveteen rabbit to a long ride in the wheelbarrow. No matter what they did, they always had a wonderful time.

The velveteen rabbit's heart was filled with joy. He loved the boy and felt lucky to spend so much time with him. The velveteen rabbit was so happy on the inside that he didn't even notice how shabby he was becoming on the outside. His fur was getting dirty from all the trips outdoors. And the space between his ears was beginning to wear thin from all the nights of being hugged and petted at bedtime.

One afternoon the boy left the velveteen rabbit hiding in the garden while he went to pick berries. Suddenly lightning flashed, and rain began to pour. The boy became frightened and ran straight home, forgetting the velveteen rabbit in the garden. At bedtime the boy realized the velveteen rabbit was still outside. Who would rescue him? Nanny, of course! The little boy looked up at the nanny with his big, sad eyes. "Will you please rescue my friend, the velveteen rabbit?" he pleaded.

Grumbling, the nanny headed outside with her flashlight. She searched in the darkness until she stumbled over the rabbit in the grass. The nanny returned with a scowl and said, "I can't believe I went out in the rain to find your silly toy!"

The boy quickly snatched the velveteen rabbit from her. "He is not a toy! He's real!" he shouted. Happy to have his friend back, the boy hugged the velveteen rabbit.

The velveteen rabbit was cold and dripping with water, but he didn't mind at all. The boy said he was real! That meant the boy loved him!

One day the boy left the velveteen rabbit on a bed of leaves. Suddenly two strange creatures appeared. They looked like the velveteen rabbit, but they could hop by themselves.

"Hello!" said one of them to the velveteen rabbit. "Would you like to come play with us?"

"N-no thank you," stuttered the velveteen rabbit. He did not want the strangers to know that he could not hop by himself.

"He's not real," said the small rabbit to his friend. "He's just a toy!" As they hopped away, the velveteen rabbit watched and wished he could follow them.

Before long the velveteen rabbit forgot all about the rabbits. He was too busy spending his time with the boy. By now, he was more tattered than ever. His plush fur was dirty and torn, and he left trails of stuffing everywhere he went. The velveteen rabbit did not seem to notice, though. When he was with the boy, he was happy, and he didn't mind how he looked.

One day something awful happened. The boy became ill, and everything changed. The velveteen rabbit became very worried.

The velveteen rabbit stayed close to the boy and did whatever he could to help him get better. He spent his days imagining all the fun they would have when the boy was well again. At night he whispered his plans to the boy. The velveteen rabbit was sure he could make him feel better.

With the help of the velveteen rabbit, the boy soon got better. Things were wonderful again. The boy and the velveteen rabbit went to the garden and played and did all the fun things they used to do. The velveteen rabbit was happier than he had ever been until the boy and his family went on vacation. The velveteen rabbit was accidentally forgotten!

The velveteen rabbit watched the boy and his family drive away. The velveteen rabbit began to cry. In the spot where his tears had fallen, a flower grew. The flower held a magical figure who said, "Hello, dear rabbit, your love for the boy has earned you the right to become real!"

"Wasn't I real already?" asked the rabbit.

"Only to the boy. Now, I will make you real to everyone!" Suddenly the rabbit could hop on his own.

When the boy returned home from his long vacation, he ran to the woods to play. As he was walking, the boy saw a rabbit who looked very familiar. His glossy fur coat had a dark patch over the left eye. The rabbit was not like all the other little rabbits who normally ran away when they saw the boy.

He hopped right up to the boy as if to say hello. The boy knelt down and smiled warmly at the friendly rabbit. "That's amazing," thought the boy. "This bunny looks just like my old friend, the velveteen rabbit."

The boy smiled as he thought of all the fun times he had shared with the velveteen rabbit. They had been on so many adventures together both during the day and in the boy's dreams. The boy did not know that his friend had returned, a real rabbit at last, and was standing right in front of him!

Though he lived in the woods now and could move on his own, the rabbit would never forget the boy's love, which had helped him become real.

Aladdin

Adapted by Brian Conway
Illustrated by Laurie Jordan

In the deserts of Persia, there lived a poor young man named Aladdin, who lived with his mother. One day while traveling through the desert, Aladdin met a finely dressed, bearded man.

"If you help me," the man said, "I'll give you a reward. I left an old lamp in this cave many years ago. Now I cannot fit through the opening. Will you go in and get the lamp for me?"

"That sounds easy," Aladdin said. "What is the reward?"

The stranger gave Aladdin a ring. "Take this for now," he said. "And when I get my lamp from you, I'll give you something better."

That ring alone was the most valuable thing Aladdin had ever seen! Aladdin gladly squeezed his way into the cave.

It was dark inside the cave. Aladdin was very frightened. "I do not see your lamp," Aladdin called. "I can't see anything in here!"

"Just keep going, boy!" the bearded man shouted.

Aladdin wondered what else might be creeping through the darkness with him. There could be snakes and spiders, he thought, and what if he stepped on a tail of a sleeping mountain lion? Aladdin stood still until he could decide what to do.

The bearded man listened for Aladdin's shuffling feet. Hearing nothing, the man said sharply, "What's the matter? Hurry up!"

The bearded man was very anxious to have that old lamp. It would give him fantastic magical powers. He was really a wicked magician from another land. The magician hid these facts from Aladdin, and he hid something else, too. Under his cloak, he held a knife, which he planned to use on Aladdin after the magic lamp was delivered safely to his hands.

Aladdin continued down the dark passage. "I can see a light now," he called back.

"Good," said the magician. Pleased with himself, he growled out a low laugh, "Very good, indeed."

Aladdin heard the bearded man's laughter echoing through the cave. The stranger could not be trusted, Aladdin thought.

"Simply follow the light and crawl to the bright cavern," the magician's voice directed him. "You will find my lamp there. Bring it to me, and you'll soon have your reward!"

The stranger laughed again. Something was not right. Aladdin stepped slowly toward the light. He had to shade his eyes as he crawled into the brightly lit cavern.

Aladdin squinted to see inside the brilliant cave. He saw a room filled with sparkling colors. "My goodness," he sighed in amazement. "I must have stepped into a giant treasure chest!"

Millions of sparkling jewels filled the cavern from top to bottom. There were diamonds, emeralds, rubies, and more remarkable stones than Aladdin could name. They hung like fruit from gold and silver trees.

In the glow of the wondrous treasure trees, Aladdin laughed and danced. His foot grazed a dull, dusty piece of metal on the ground. "Ah, the old lamp," Aladdin whispered. "What would the strange man want with this old thing?"

Aladdin took one last look as he left the room of magnificent jewels. Holding the lamp behind him, he headed back to the door. Aladdin wondered why the bearded man preferred the dusty old lamp to a room of treasure. Aladdin was suspicious.

"I have found your lamp," he called through the doorway.

"What took you so long?" the magician asked angrily. "Give me my lamp!"

"First give me the reward you promised," Aladdin answered.

"Step out here, my good friend," the magician urged him.

Aladdin took a step back instead. "Come in here," he answered, "and bring me my reward. Then you will get your old lamp!"

Because of an ancient magic spell, the wicked magician could not step foot inside the cave. He became very angry.

"Ungrateful boy!" he shouted. "If you do not give me the lamp, I will close this cave forever!"

Aladdin refused again. The magician muttered a magic spell, and the stone rolled over the cave door. Aladdin was trapped! He sat alone in the darkness. His thoughts turned to his poor mother as a tear fell onto the dusty old lamp.

Aladdin rubbed the tears from his eyes. With his cloak, he wiped the lamp dry. As he rubbed the lamp, it began to shake. Frightened, Aladdin dropped it. A brilliant stream of sparkling light rose from the lamp's spout and a genie appeared.

"I am the Genie of the Lamp," he said. "Wish for anything, and I will make your wishes come true!"

Amazed, Aladdin struggled to speak, but he knew what he wanted most. "Get me out of this awful cave," he said.

"Your wish is my command," the genie said as he clapped his hands. Instantly the stone rolled away from the door. "Because you freed me from the lamp, I will grant your every wish."

Aladdin's mind raced. "Anything?" he asked excitedly. "Well, I always wanted some fine new clothes."

"Your wish is my command, Master Aladdin," the genie said. He clapped his hands again, and suddenly Aladdin was covered in the handsome costume of a wealthy prince!

"Now I would like to go home to see my mother," Aladdin said.

"Your wish is my command," the genie said again. He clapped his hands, and a magic carpet lifted Aladdin high into the air!

Soaring on the magic carpet, Aladdin swiftly returned home to his mother. Excitedly, he explained what had happened that day. He rubbed the magic lamp, and the genie appeared.

"I am the Genie of the Lamp," he said again. "Wish for anything, and I will make your wishes come true!"

Taking his mother by the hand, Aladdin said, "We need a new house." He saw his mother smile more widely than he'd ever seen before. "It should have steps of gold, and pillars of pure silver, and windows made of diamonds," Aladdin continued. "Build it in the city, beside the sultan's palace."

"Your wish is my command," said the genie. He clapped his hands and disappeared in a flash. In a few moments he returned.

"Your new home is ready, Master Aladdin," the genie said.

Aladdin and his mother climbed on the magic carpet and flew to the city. Their new home had everything they ever wanted.

Aladdin's house of treasures made the sultan's palace look like a tiny hut! The sultan himself wondered about his wealthy new neighbors, and his lovely daughter, the princess, wished to meet the handsome prince who lived there.

The next day Aladdin received an invitation to dine at the sultan's palace. He had a special gift in mind for the sultan. He gathered the jewels he'd taken from the cave.

When Aladdin arrived at the palace that evening, servants led him to the sultan's banquet room. Aladdin puffed out his chest and walked straight and tall, the way he thought a prince should walk. Aladdin presented himself as Aladdin Ali-Abu, a prince from a faraway land.

"Come, Prince Aladdin," said the sultan. "Join us for dinner."

The princess entered and sat beside her father. Aladdin's gaze was drawn to her, as hers was to the young prince.

"First I have a present for you," Aladdin said to the sultan. "Please accept these jewels from my homeland."

The sultan had never seen jewels like these before! They were spectacular! He thought Aladdin must be very rich indeed.

Aladdin picked a gem from the pile. He handed it to the princess, saying, "And the most brilliant, beautiful gem goes to the princess, the most perfect lady in the land!"

The princess smiled, and the sultan was pleased.

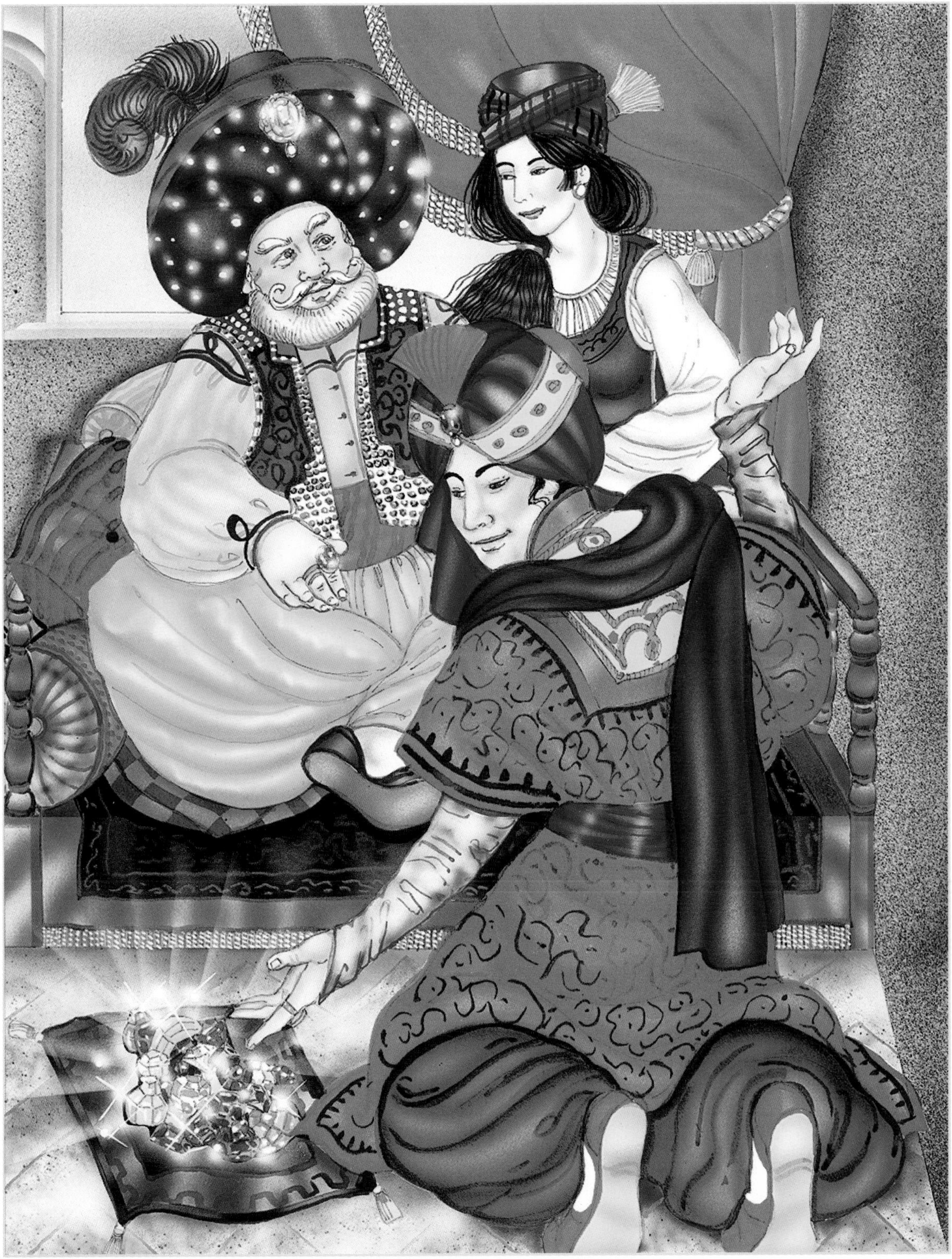

Later that evening when the princess had gone, Aladdin boldly asked the sultan for his daughter's hand in marriage.

"But you've only just met!" said the surprised sultan. "I still do not know if you are a worthy prince."

"You have seen my riches," said Aladdin. "Anything your daughter wants, I will provide for her."

"To marry the princess you will have to do better than a handful of gems," said the sultan. He then thought of a difficult task. "Tomorrow bring me forty bags of gold in a silver carriage pulled by the finest horse in Persia. Maybe then will I consider your offer."

Encouraged by the sultan's promise, Aladdin hurried home to his magic lamp and told the genie, "I want to marry the princess."

"Your wish is m—," the genie stopped. He sighed, "But, Master, even my magic cannot make someone fall in love."

"First I must convince her father," said Aladdin. "Listen to what I must bring him."

Hearing the request, the genie clapped his hands. Instantly there appeared forty bags of gold in a silver carriage pulled by the finest horse in Persia.

The next day Aladdin led the horse and carriage to his neighbor's palace. The sultan met him in the garden. "You did it!" the sultan chuckled. "You truly are a wealthy prince! You may marry my daughter, as long as it is her wish as well."

The princess watched from her balcony. She was not impressed by gold and silver, but she was impressed by the prince's generosity. She went to visit Aladdin in the garden.

"I gave your father forty bags of gold," Aladdin said boldly, as he thought a prince would do. "Now what do you wish for?"

"My wish is simple," said the princess. "I wish for true love."

Taking her hand, Aladdin said, "Your wish is my command." Aladdin did not need the magic of the lamp to grant her that wish. "I will love you with all my heart," he told the princess.

The princess happily agreed to marry Aladdin. For a wedding present, Aladdin asked the genie to build them a magnificent palace. "We will be surrounded by many wonderful things," Aladdin told her, "but our love will soar above them all."

The happy couple climbed aboard the magic carpet and soared away to their new home.

The Ugly Duckling

Adapted by Sarah Toast

Illustrated by Susan Spellman

Once upon a time, on a spring day in the country, something exciting was about to happen. A mother duck was sitting on her nest by the edge of a pond. She had been sitting there for a very long time waiting for her eggs to hatch.

Finally the eggs began to crack. "Peep, peep," said the newly hatched ducklings. "Quack, quack," said their mother. "You are the sweetest little yellow ducklings that I have ever seen! Are you all here?" She stood up to look in the nest. She saw that the biggest egg hadn't hatched yet.

The tired mother duck sat down again on the last egg. When it finally cracked open, out tumbled a clumsy, gray baby bird.

The gray duckling was bigger than the others, and he didn't look like them. In fact, compared to the other baby ducks, he was rather funny looking.

"Peep, peep," said the big, gray baby. The mother duck looked at him. "He's awfully big for his age," she thought to herself. "His neck is a little too long and his feet are a bit too big. I wonder if he can swim?"

The next day the sun shone brightly. The mother duck led her ducklings to the pond. "Quack, quack," she told them, and the ducklings understood. One after the other, the eager ducklings jumped into the water. They bobbed and floated like little corks. They knew how to paddle their legs and swim without being told.

All the new baby birds swam very nicely, even the one who looked different. "He may have too long a neck," thought the mother duck, "but see how nicely he holds it. If you tilt your head a little bit, he is almost handsome." For the rest of the afternoon, the mother duck helped all the baby ducklings practice their swimming.

The mother duck was very happy with her ducklings. She decided it was time to take her babies to the farm to meet the other ducks. "Quack, quack," said the mother duck. "Follow me! Keep your legs far apart and waddle."

The yellow ducklings knew exactly what to do. "Peep, peep," they answered their mother. One by one they waddled behind their mother just as she had shown them. They walked all the way to the farm yard.

The big, gray baby could not quite get it right. But he did not give up. He followed the others to the farm, doing his best to keep up. When they arrived at the farm, the other ducks gathered around him and said, "Look how ugly that duckling is!" One big duck came over and quacked, "Stay out of my way, you ugly duckling!"

"Leave him alone!" cried the mother duck. "He may not be so handsome, but he does his best and can swim as well as anyone—maybe even better!" No one listened to her. The other ducks acted mean and chased the poor ugly duckling.

A few days later, the other ducklings were playing on the farm. They wouldn't let the ugly duckling join in any of the games. "Go away, you ugly duckling!" they said to him. This made the little duckling very sad. For a while, he sat all alone.

But the ugly duckling did not want to feel sorry for himself. He had an idea. "I can practice my swimming!" he said to himself.

The ugly duckling went to the pond and swam and swam and swam. When he stopped, he was very tired. Then he looked around. The ugly duckling had no idea where he was!

What was that noise? A big hunting dog walked along the shore. The dog scouted out the area very near the ugly duckling! The scared duckling tried to make himself as small as possible. He was so afraid to move that he stayed in the water all night.

When morning came, the ugly duckling was sure the dog had gone away. But just to be certain, the duckling carefully looked around. The dog was indeed gone, but the baby duck was still lost. Now he was hungry, too, and even a little bit scared. The duckling knew he needed to do something.

"I'll just have to try to find something to eat," said the ugly duckling. He hopped out of the pond and looked around. There was a farm down the road. He waddled closer to take a look. Near the farmhouse he saw a woman. "Peep," said the duckling.

The woman said, "You look hungry. Come get something to eat." When they got inside the house, the ugly duckling saw a cat and a pet hen. The cat and hen stared right at the ugly duckling. The duckling stared at the floor.

The duckling couldn't lay eggs like the hen or purr like the cat. They picked on him because he was different. After a few days, the duckling remembered how much he liked to be in the fresh air and how much he missed swimming in the water. One night he quietly left the house.

The duckling waddled farther down the road and soon found a lake where other wild ducks lived. In this lake the duckling could dive to the bottom and pop back up again to float. The swimming helped him grow bigger and stronger. Still, none of the wild ducks would talk to him because they thought he was too ugly.

Soon the seasons changed. It was fall now. The leaves turned colors, and the air got cooler. The duckling found that the water was getting colder, too. One evening, just at sunset, a flock of beautiful birds flew overhead. Their feathers were shiny white, and they had long, graceful necks. The birds were flying south to find a warmer place to live for the winter.

The ugly duckling stretched his neck as far as he could to look at the beautiful birds. He felt sad as he watched them. He wished he could fly away with them. Soon he was shivering, and he felt very lonely.

Winter came, and the pond turned to ice. A duck cannot swim on ice. The ugly duckling needed to practice, so he went in search of water that wasn't frozen.

Soon he came to a farmhouse. The fireplace had a roaring fire in it. Everything inside looked very warm and cozy. He waddled into the house and began his search. Finally he found something. It was much smaller than the pond, but it would just have to do. He jumped in and started to swim.

The farmer's wife heard a lot of splashing. She ran to the sound immediately. She was very surprised to find a large bird inside the house! She quickly grabbed the broom and chased him back out into the snow, knocking over a fresh bucket of milk in the process. Her two children laughed and laughed at the big bird who had tried to swim in their bathtub.

The duckling was really scared now! He found a hiding place under some bushes. Snow fell all around him as he did his very best to stay warm.

The poor ugly duckling had a hard time that long winter. There was barely any food to eat, and the icy wind made him very cold. But just when he thought he couldn't stand it any more, something wonderful happened—spring arrived! Suddenly there was warm sunshine and blooming flowers. Many birds came back from their winter homes.

It was now warm enough to go back on the lake. Anxious to swim again, the ugly duckling dove into the water. How good it felt to swim in the water again!

The ugly duckling stretched his neck all around. His wings felt so strong. When he looked down, what a surprise he got!

There in the water was the most beautiful bird he had ever seen. It had a long, graceful neck and elegant wings. He looked at the swans swimming farther down the lake. The ugly duckling jumped when one of them called, "Come join us."

"What? Could this be true?" the ugly duckling said to himself. "Could the beautiful swans really be talking to me?"

The ugly duckling looked down in the water again. Why, that wasn't another bird at all. It was his own reflection that he saw in the water. Over the winter the ugly duckling had grown into a beautiful swan. He really wasn't a duck at all. No wonder he didn't fit in.

The other swans circled around him and stroked him with their beaks. All the young swan had gone through made him appreciate his newfound happiness. He saw beauty in everything around him. He ruffled his feathers and thought, "I never dreamed I could be so happy when I was an ugly duckling."

Rumpelstiltskin

Adapted by Jane Jerrard
Illustrated by Burgandy Nilles

Once there was a poor miller who lived with his daughter. The miller was in the habit of boasting to anyone who would listen of his daughter's great beauty and talents.

One day, on his way to deliver flour to the castle, the miller happened to meet the king. The miller immediately started bragging about his daughter. He told the king that she was the most beautiful, talented maiden in the land.

The king just yawned. The boastful miller was very determined to have the king notice his daughter. So he bragged on. "I've saved the best for last, your majesty. My daughter can even spin straw into gold!"

"Straw into gold?" said the king. "Now that is indeed a talent."

The king was a very greedy man, so he ordered the miller to bring his daughter to the castle.

"If it is true what you say about your daughter," the king told the miller, "she will be very useful to me. Bring her to me, and I will find out if you speak the truth." The king rode off toward the castle, and the miller called after him.

"Yes, your majesty," he said as he bowed down. "Thank you, your majesty."

The miller left his daughter there at the castle, and the king took the girl to a room filled with straw. He told his servants to bring in a spinning wheel.

"Now get to work," said the king. "If you do not spin this straw into gold by morning, you will die."

Sadly what the miller had told the king about his daughter was not true. The poor girl knew how to spin flax and wool, but she could not spin straw into gold. She was so frightened that she began to cry. Suddenly the locked door flew open and there stood a strange little man.

"Good evening, pretty maid," he said. "Why are you crying so?"

The miller's daughter was very surprised to see such a strange little man in her spinning room.

"My father boasted to the king that I can spin straw into gold. But you see, I cannot. Now surely I must die," she wept.

The little man picked up a bit of straw and examined it. He twirled it in his tiny fingers. He tugged at it with his tiny hands. He even sniffed at it with his little round nose. Then he smiled at the weeping girl.

"Dry your tears, my lady. I shall have no trouble spinning this straw into gold. What will you give me if I do this for you?" he asked the maiden.

"I will give you my necklace," she replied.

The odd little man took the necklace and sat down at the wheel. He picked up straw and began to spin. By morning the spools held spun gold, and the man was gone.

When the greedy king entered the room in the morning, he was greatly pleased to see the gold. That evening the king took the maiden to a bigger room filled with even more straw. Once again he commanded her to spin all the straw into gold if she valued her life.

Locked in the room, the girl sat down and began to weep.
How would she save herself this time? The room was filled with
straw she could not spin into gold. But soon the strange little man
appeared once again.

"Dry your tears, my lady. What will you give me if I spin this
straw into gold?" he asked.

"I will give you my ring," she replied.

So the little man took the ring, started the spinning wheel
whirring, and by morning he had spun all the straw into bright gold.

But the king was still not satisfied. He sent the girl to a larger
room filled with straw to the ceiling. Then he promised to marry
her if she could spin that straw into gold. The girl did not really
want to marry such a greedy king, but she knew she would be
killed if she did not do as he asked. And so she agreed.

That night the strange little man came for the third time and
asked what the girl would give him if he helped her.

"I have nothing to give you," she said.

"Then give me your firstborn child when you become queen,"
the little man replied.

The girl thought this was a very strange request, but she did not know what the future held. She agreed to give the little man her firstborn child. By morning the room was filled with gold.

The king married the miller's daughter, and she became queen. After that the king became much kinder and never asked her to spin straw into gold again.

One year later the queen gave birth to a beautiful child. She loved her baby so much that she forgot all about her agreement with the strange little man. But one day he appeared while the baby slept.

"I spun all of your straw into gold. I helped you become the queen. Now give me what you promised me the last time we met," he demanded.

The young queen was horrified. She loved her baby dearly and could not give it up. "I'll give you anything else you want," she cried, "but do not take my child!"

The little man felt some pity for the queen, so he told her, "I will give you three days and nights to guess my name. If you can guess it, you can keep your child."

The queen thought she would have no trouble guessing the little man's name in three days. She sat up all night making a long list of names. When the little man came to her the next day, she asked, "Is it Caspar, Melchior, or Balthazar?"

But for each one the little man grinned and said, "No, that is not my name."

"Alex, Abraham, or Aloysius? Boris, Bruce, or Brian? Casey, Chris, or Carlos?" asked the queen hopefully.

"No, no, and no again!" he answered with every name the queen read.

The queen began to worry. "Is it Dudley, Davis, or Draco? Enos, Edward, or Eucleides?" she asked. But she simply could not guess his name.

By the end of the first day, the queen had tried all the names on her list with no luck. As the strange little man left that day he called out, "Only two more days left!"

The queen was terribly worried. She quickly sent messengers to all four corners of the kingdom and asked them to bring back the strangest names they could find.

When the messengers returned from their search, the queen wrote a new list of names. The second day she tried them all.

"Could you be Ribcage, Muttonchop, or Lacelegs? Are you Hercules or Xerxes?"

"Of course not," he said.

"What about Socrates or Soapsuds? Heathcliff, Bustopher, or Beauregarde?" asked the queen desperately. But she could not guess his name.

"Only one day left!" the little man giggled gleefully as he skipped away.

After he left, the queen sent twice as many messengers as the day before to find her more names. As the last messenger was returning, he made his way through a small wood near the castle. There he came upon a little man dancing around a fire and singing,

> *Today I brew, and then I bake,*
>
> *And then the queen's own child I'll take.*
>
> *For little knows my royal dame*
>
> *That Rumpelstiltskin is my name!*

The messenger rushed back to the castle and told the queen what he had heard. The queen cried out with joy and rewarded the messenger well. Then she prepared a final list of names for the little man, saving his own for last. When the smug little man returned later that day, the queen was ready.

"Is your name Kurt or Bert?"

"No, it is not."

"Tom, Dick, or Harry?"

"Wrong again."

"Could it be Groucho or Harpo?

"No! Your time is up, my queen. Now give me the baby!" shouted the little man.

"Wait just a minute. I have one final guess," said the queen. "Is your name, by any chance, Rumpelstiltskin?"

The little man was completely amazed and stared at the queen for a long moment. Then he screamed out in rage, "How did you know it? No one could ever possibly have guessed it!"

The strange little man was so furious that he stamped his feet right through the floor and disappeared forever.

The North Wind

Adapted by Sarah Toast
Illustrated by Sharron O'Neil

Long ago in a northern land, a little boy lived with his mother. One day the boy bought some oats for his mother. As he walked home, the cold North Wind swept down upon him. With one great windy puff, the North Wind blew away all the oats.

The boy was sad when he got home. He and his mother had no money left to buy more oats. The boy decided to visit the North Wind and try to get the oats back.

It was a long walk to the North Wind's house. It was cold and the boy grew afraid. By the time he arrived, his hand shook so hard that it knocked on the door by itself. Immediately the door swung open. Out blew the North Wind.

"What is it you want?" asked the North Wind gruffly.

The boy was afraid of the grumpy North Wind, but he gathered up his courage. "I have come to ask you to give back our oats," he said. "My mother and I do not have much to eat, and now our money is gone as well."

"I can't give back your oats," said the North Wind. "They have been scattered to the winds. But you and your mother are poor, and you were brave to come here. For this, I will give you a magic tablecloth."

The North Wind told the boy to lay the cloth on the table and say "Cloth, cloth! Serve up food!" The cloth would make all the food that he and his mother could eat. The boy was very pleased with the gift. He thanked the North Wind and set off for home with the cloth.

When it began to get dark, the boy decided to spend the night at an inn. He laid the cloth on a table in the dining room and said, "Cloth, cloth! Serve up food!" The innkeeper was amazed to see all the delicious food appear. He wanted to keep the tablecloth for himself.

After the boy fell asleep, the innkeeper crept up the stairs. He carried an ordinary tablecloth that looked just like the magic one. He entered the boy's room and traded the magic cloth for the plain one.

In the morning the boy took the cloth and walked the rest of the way home. When he burst through the door, he shouted to his mother, "Mother, come quickly! The North Wind has given us a magic cloth. It will give us all the food we need! We will never need to buy oats again."

The mother replied, "Seeing is believing. Show me what the cloth does."

The boy pulled the magic cloth from his basket. He proudly laid the cloth on their little kitchen table and said, "Cloth, cloth! Serve up food!" Nothing happened. The boy couldn't believe his eyes. Not even a crust of bread appeared on the table, no matter how many times the boy said the magic words. He and his mother went hungry that day.

The next morning the boy made up his mind to go back to the North Wind and tell him that the cloth didn't work.

It was a long walk back to the home of the North Wind. The wind howled through the woods as the boy bravely walked alone. By the time he reached the North Wind's home, he was very tired and even a little bit scared to complain about the magic cloth.

When the boy knocked on the door, the North Wind appeared just as gruffly as before. "I see you've come back again," growled the North Wind. "What do you want from me now?"

"I've come to tell you that you took our oats, and the cloth you gave us doesn't serve food." The boy shivered a little as he spoke. "My mother and I are still very hungry."

"I don't have another magic cloth, and I don't have any oats," said the North Wind. "But I do have a piggy bank that I can give you. If you say, 'Piggy bank, piggy bank! Make money!' it will give you all the money you need."

"Thank you," said the boy. "My mother will be so pleased." Smiling, the boy accepted the magic bank and immediately departed for home.

It was already late when he reached the inn, so he decided to stop there again.

The innkeeper welcomed the boy. He was eager to see if the boy had other magic treasures like the cloth. Cold and hungry from traveling, the boy sat down at a table near the fire. The innkeeper brought him a delicious feast.

When the time came to pay for his dinner, the boy set the piggy bank on the table and said, "Piggy bank, piggy bank! Make money!" Then he reached into the piggy bank and pulled out enough coins to pay the innkeeper for dinner and a room for the night.

The innkeeper was amazed at the sight. This piggy bank was even more wonderful than the table cloth!

After dinner the boy went right upstairs to bed. He was sound asleep when the innkeeper crept into the room with an ordinary piggy bank under his arm. He took the boy's magic piggy bank and left the ordinary one in its place.

The next morning when the boy reached home, he happily told his mother that the North Wind had given them a magic piggy bank. "I'll believe it when I see it work," said his mother. When the boy said "Piggy bank, piggy bank! Make money!" not one coin came out of the bank.

The boy and his mother had no food left and no money. The boy was afraid to visit the grumpy North Wind again, but he knew he had to get help.

Once more the boy set out on the long walk to the home of the North Wind. This time the North Wind was angrier than ever. He wanted the boy to stop bothering him, and the North Wind opened the door before the boy even knocked.

"Well, what do you want now?" roared the North Wind with his icy breath.

The boy respectfully removed his hat. He was very scared, but he knew he had to help his mother. Doing his best to be brave, he said, "I must get my oats back," said the boy. "The piggy bank doesn't work."

"I have only one thing left," said the North Wind. "It is a rope." The North Wind pointed to a rope that hung on the wall. "This is a magic rope. It will tie someone up if you say 'Rope, rope! Tie him up!' Because you have bravely come all this way, I will give it to you."

The boy thanked the North Wind and set out for home again.

By now the boy had figured out what had happened to his magic cloth and his piggy bank, so he had an idea what to do with the magic rope.

When he reached the inn on the way home, the boy again stopped for the night. Cold as ever, he sat down at a table near the fire. Although he didn't have any money, the innkeeper gave him a delicious dinner and a place to sleep.

As the boy ate, the innkeeper stared at the ordinary looking rope. Surely that rope must be magic, too, he thought. The greedy innkeeper made a plan to steal it.

After dinner the boy went right upstairs to bed, but this time he only pretended to go to sleep.

Later the innkeeper crept into the boy's room to replace the magic rope with an ordinary rope. But the boy was ready for him this time. When he came close to the boy's bed, the boy sprang up and shouted, "Rope, rope! Tie him up!" The magic rope sprung from its place on the bedpost and wrapped around the innkeeper. Around and around the rope went until the innkeeper was no longer able to move.

The innkeeper struggled but could not get loose. "Let me go!" he shouted.

The boy said, "I won't untie you until you give me back my magic cloth and piggy bank!"

The innkeeper struggled some more, but at last he said, "Take them back! Just set me free!"

The boy commanded the rope to set the innkeeper free. Magically, the rope unwound itself and fell to the floor. Afraid of being caught again, the innkeeper immediately fetched the cloth and piggy bank.

With his magic things in hand, the boy returned home. He was more excited than ever to show them to his mother. This time when she said, "Seeing is believing," everything worked as the boy expected.

Over time the cloth provided them with plenty of food, and the piggy bank gave them money to meet their needs. In case they ever needed its help, the rope was nearby to protect them.

The boy went to see the North Wind one last time—to thank him for his help. This time he was not afraid at all.

Little Red Riding Hood

Adapted by Jane Jerrard
Illustrated by Susan Spellman

There was once a little girl who lived in a village at the edge of a large forest. The girl's grandmother lived in a house deep in the forest. The grandmother loved the girl more than kittens love mischief and had made her a beautiful red cloak with a hood. The little girl wore the velvet riding cloak everywhere she went. She wore it so often that the other villagers called her Little Red Riding Hood.

One day, when Little Red Riding Hood was out picking flowers, her mother called her to the house. "I just heard that Grandmother is sick," said the mother. "I am worried about her being all alone."

"I know a way to make Grandmother feel much better," said Little Red Riding Hood's mother. "Please put down your flowers and come inside."

Little Red Riding Hood and her mother spent the day baking fresh bread, tasty muffins, and sweet cakes for Little Red Riding Hood's grandmother.

The next morning Little Red Riding Hood's mother put all the delicious food into a basket and called Little Red Riding Hood into the kitchen.

"I would like you to bring this food to Grandmother's house. I'm sure a visit with you will make her feel much better." Little Red Riding Hood happily agreed and put on her hooded cloak.

"You must be very careful going through the woods all by yourself," said her mother. "You must stay on the open path and walk quickly and quietly. Be careful not to stumble and drop the basket of food."

"I will be very careful," promised Little Red Riding Hood. She waved good-bye and started down the path through the woods to her grandmother's house.

Little Red Riding Hood had a wonderful time on her walk through the woods. Always staying on the path, she skipped along and chased butterflies.

It was not long before Little Red Riding Hood met a wolf on the path. She had never seen a wolf before and did not know that wolves can be very mean and hungry. The wolf looked friendly to her, so Little Red Riding Hood was not a bit afraid.

"Good morning," said the wolf. "Where are you going this fine day, little girl?"

"I'm going to my grandmother's house under the three big oak trees," she answered. "I'm bringing her a basket of food to make her feel better." She lifted the towel from the basket to show the wolf the goodies inside.

The wolf licked his chops. The cakes and muffins looked tasty, but he thought Little Red Riding Hood would make an even better snack. Still someone might come along the path any minute. So he slyly said he was going her way.

"May I walk with you?" he asked in his most gentlemanly wolfish voice.

"Of course! It's always nice to have someone to walk with me," Little Red Riding Hood replied. She walked quickly just as her mother had told her to do. She did not want to be too late in arriving at her grandmother's house.

Meanwhile the sneaky wolf was busy thinking up a plan.

"Just look at those wildflowers at the side of the path!" he said. "Wouldn't it do your grandmother good to have a bouquet of fresh flowers?"

The girl looked around her and saw the sunlight dancing on the flowers. Surely it couldn't hurt to take just one step off the path to pick some flowers for Grandmother. She gathered a small bouquet.

"And look at those ripe strawberries on the other side!" said the wolf. "Wouldn't your grandmother love some juicy berries?"

Little Red Riding Hood thought the strawberries looked very ripe and delicious. She decided to pick a few for Grandmother. But one patch of strawberries led to another, and soon Little Red Riding Hood had gone far from the path. She didn't notice that the wolf was no longer waiting for her.

While Little Red Riding Hood was busy picking strawberries, the tricky wolf went on ahead to look for Grandmother's house. He found it just where Little Red Riding Hood had said it was, under the three big oak trees.

"My plan is working perfectly," chuckled the wolf. "And I shall have a Little Red Riding Hood for my lunch!"

The wolf knocked on Grandmother's front door.

"Who's there?" Grandmother called.

The sly wolf answered in a high voice, "It is Little Red Riding Hood. I have brought you a basket of goodies!"

"Lift the latch, child," said Grandmother. "I am ill and cannot get out of bed."

The hungry wolf lifted the latch, leaped through the door, and frightened poor Grandmother right out of bed.

"You are not Little Red Riding Hood at all!" Grandmother cried. She ran to the cupboard and locked herself inside. The wolf then found Grandmother's lacy cap and nightgown. He put them on, climbed into her bed, and pulled the covers up to his chin. Then he waited.

By now Little Red Riding Hood had picked a beautiful bouquet of flowers and plenty of strawberries and found her way back to the path.

"Oh dear, this took longer than I thought," said Little Red Riding Hood. "I hope I am not too late with Grandmother's lunch!" She quickly walked the rest of the way and knocked on her grandmother's door.

"Who's there?" called the wolf, as he tried to make his voice sound like Grandmother's.

"It is Little Red Riding Hood, Grandmother," said the little girl. "I have brought a wonderful basket of goodies to help make you feel better."

"Lift the latch, child," said the wolf in a grandmotherly voice. "I cannot get out of bed."

Little Red Riding Hood went inside, and wished a good morning to her grandmother. For a few minutes she kept herself busy by arranging the flowers in a jug and finding a big bowl for the strawberries. She also got out some plates and put the bread and muffins and cakes on the table.

Finally Little Red Riding Hood went over to Grandmother's bed to give her a kiss on the cheek. But when she came close, Little Red Riding Hood gasped. Grandmother looked so odd that Little Red Riding Hood felt frightened. She stared at Grandmother for a long moment.

"Oh, Grandmother," she said at last, her eyes wide. "What big ears you have!"

"The better to hear you with, my dear," said the wolf, in a grandmotherly voice. Little Red Riding Hood looked still closer at her grandmother.

"And Grandmother, what big eyes you have," said Little Red Riding Hood.

"The better to see you with, my dear," he replied. Little Red Riding Hood peered again at her grandmother.

"But Grandmother, what big teeth you have," said Little Red Riding Hood.

"The better to eat you with, my dear!" cried the wolf as he jumped out of bed. Little Red Riding Hood shrieked and ran from the wolf.

As the wolf chased Little Red Riding Hood around and around the room, he tripped on the hem of Grandmother's long nightgown. But even in a nightgown, he was a very quick wolf. Despite his clumsiness, the wolf finally trapped Little Red Riding Hood in a corner.

"I think I am ready for my lunch!" growled the wolf, licking his chops.

But as good luck would have it, the wolf had trapped Little Red Riding Hood in the corner where Grandmother was hiding in the cupboard.

All this time Grandmother had been waiting for the right moment to save Little Red Riding Hood. Just when the wolf was getting ready to pounce, Grandmother flung the cupboard door open with all her might and knocked the wolf off his feet.

As soon as Grandmother knocked over the wolf, Little Red Riding Hood had a chance to run out the door and away from the house.

"Help! Help! The wolf is after me!" shouted Little Red Riding Hood.

As Little Red Riding Hood ran down the path crying for help, a hunter heard her calls. He had been tracking this mischievous wolf for days and had noticed the paw prints on the path leading to Grandmother's house.

"This will be the end of that tricky wolf," said the hunter, hiding behind one of Grandmother's bushes.

The angry wolf dashed out of the house after Little Red Riding Hood, still wearing Grandmother's cap and nightgown. The hunter took careful aim with his rifle. He fired one shot, and the wolf fell dead.

As soon as the hunter shot the wolf, Little Red Riding Hood turned right around and ran back into the house to look for her grandmother. Inside, she found her leaning shakily against the cupboard.

Grandmother and Little Red Riding Hood invited the hunter in to thank him. They sat down to enjoy some baked goodies and had a very nice visit. Soon Grandmother felt much better.

As the kind hunter walked Little Red Riding Hood home, she said to herself that she would never stray from the path again.

Peter Pan

Adapted by Lisa Harkrader
Illustrated by Sam Thiewes

Sometimes, when the night is velvet black and the stars are diamond bright, you will see one star glittering brighter than the rest. It will flit about the night sky, skipping and twirling. Then if you sit very still, you will hear a tiny, silver tinkling. From this you will know fairies are at play.

On just such a night not so very long ago, Mrs. Darling tucked her children, Wendy, John, and Michael, into their beds. She settled into the rocker to tell them a story. Mrs. Darling leaned in close. Wendy, Michael, and John shut their eyes.

Only Nana, their faithful dog, saw the boy listening at the window. Only Nana heard the tinkling and twinkling of the fairy.

The boy pressed on the glass, and the window swung open. Nana leaped to her feet. The boy and the fairy saw Nana bounding toward them. They darted out into the night. But the boy's shadow was not as quick. When Nana slammed the window shut, the shadow remained in a rumpled heap on the nursery room floor.

Mrs. Darling finished the story and turned out the light. As soon as she left the nursery, the boy tapped on the glass. Wendy, John, and Michael sat up in bed.

"My shadow!" The boy pointed through the glass. Wendy unlatched the window for the boy and the fairy. "I'm Peter Pan," said the boy, "and I've come for my shadow." He stared down at it and frowned. "But look—it's a wrinkled mess." He poked the shadow with his toe. "And how will I ever get it back on?"

"Easy," said Wendy. She picked up the shadow, gave it a good shake, and laid it on the floor at Peter's feet. "Stand still," she told him as she opened her sewing kit. She smoothed out the creases, brushed off Nana's paw prints, and began stitching it to Peter's shoes. Peter twitched and giggled, but soon Wendy was finished. She tied a knot and snipped the thread.

Peter bounced on the bed, somersaulted over the dresser, and began flying about the room. His shadow followed, limply at first, then it straightened itself out and sailed along like a proper shadow. The fairy, whose name was Tinker Bell, flitted beside him.

John and Michael tried flying. They bounced on their beds—and landed with a thud on the rug. Peter giggled. He borrowed fairy dust from Tinker Bell and sprinkled it on Wendy, John, and Michael. All three leaped into the air and flew up to the ceiling.

"In Neverland you don't need fairy dust," said Peter. "In Neverland you can do anything if you believe you can."

"Neverland?" asked Wendy. "I've never heard of it."

"It's my home," said Peter, "and it's filled with pirates."

"Pirates?" cried John. "Will you take us there?"

Peter nodded.

"Can we, Wendy?" asked Michael. "Please?"

"Will we be back by morning?" asked Wendy.

"If you like," said Peter.

Wendy unlatched the window. Nana whimpered as the three children flew out into the night, led by Tinker Bell and Peter.

They swooped through the treetops and circled the moon. Peter pointed to lights in the distance. "That's Neverland," he said. "The Lost Boys are waiting."

"Lost Boys?" asked Wendy.

Peter nodded. "They were lost as babies and have no mothers."

"No mothers?" asked Wendy. "That's awful."

"Not so awful." Peter stuck his chin out. "We do what we like. Only, we don't have anyone to tell us stories. That's why I was listening at your window. I wanted to bring a story home to Neverland. Except now I can't. I didn't hear the ending."

"That's okay," said Michael. "Wendy knows the ending."

John nodded. "But right now I want to hear about pirates. Are they big and fierce? Are you afraid of them?"

"They're big and fierce," said Peter, "but we aren't afraid. Not much. Captain Hook is their leader. I cut off his arm in a duel. Now he has a hook for an arm. He's vowed to capture me."

They were directly over the lights of Neverland. As they prepared to land, a volley of arrows shot up toward them. One of the rubber tips hit Wendy. She plummeted to the ground.

John, Michael, and Peter found Wendy lying in a pile of leaves, surrounded by boys holding bows and arrows. "I'm okay," she gulped, sitting up. "I've had the wind knocked out of me."

"This is Wendy," said Peter to the Lost Boys. "She'll tell you a story while I look for the crocodile."

"The crocodile?" Wendy gasped, still catching her breath.

"If you want to get home by morning," said Peter, "I have to find the crocodile. When I cut off Hook's arm," explained Peter, "I flung it overboard. The crocodile gobbled it up."

"Captain Hook's watch was still on that arm," added a Lost Boy.

"Now it's ticking away in the croc's belly," said another.

"Hook's scared senseless of the crocodile," said Peter. "The sound of ticking drives him mad. He threw all the clocks and watches into the sea. To tell time I have to listen to the crocodile till Hook's watch chimes the hour. I'll be back soon."

Peter set off through the forest. The Lost Boys gathered around as Wendy began to tell the story of Cinderella.

When she was almost finished, a deep voice growled, "I can't wait to hear the ending." It was Captain Hook!

Pirates leaped from the trees and darted from behind rocks. Wendy and the boys tried to run, but they were surrounded. The pirates captured everyone but Tinker Bell, who hid in the treetops. As the pirates marched Wendy and the boys through the forest toward the pirate ship, Tinker Bell flew off to warn Peter.

She found the crocodile first. He was slinking along the seashore, snapping his jaws and thrashing his tail. He turned his head from side to side, hunting for a snack. With every step he took, his great leathery belly ticked.

Peter crept along behind, hidden by seaweed. Tinker Bell flew down and told him about the pirates. Peter gazed past the crocodile at the pirate ship anchored in the harbor. "Too bad the crocodile isn't on our side," he said. "If that croc boarded the pirate ship, Hook would take one look and jump into the sea."

The crocodile ambled down the shore. His belly began to chime midnight.

Peter stared at him. "Maybe the croc can help us." He smiled. "Come on, Tink. We have just enough time to save our friends and get them home before their mother wakes up."

Tinker Bell flew ahead to spy on the pirates. Peter began the long swim across the harbor. He practiced ticking until he sounded just like Hook's watch in the belly of the crocodile.

"Tick, tick, tick." Peter paddled toward the ship. The closer he got, the louder he ticked. "Tick, tick, tick."

"Do you hear something?" he heard one of the pirates ask.

"Sounds like that crocodile," said another.

"We should warn the captain," said the first pirate.

Peter heard the pirates scuffle off. He climbed onto the ship, ticking as he went, and hid between some barrels and trunks. Tinker Bell darted down from her post high in the sails. She told him Hook had given Wendy and the boys a choice—he would spare their lives if they would become pirates. Wendy and the boys had refused, of course. They were tied up on deck. Soon the captain would force them to walk the plank.

Peter peeked out from his hiding place. He could see the pirates huddled together at one end of the ship, Captain Hook in the very middle. Peter ticked louder as he crept around the deck toward the children.

Peter untied Wendy and the boys. They all began ticking as they tiptoed toward the pirates. Thinking there were hundreds of crocodiles, all the pirates scrambled overboard and swam toward shore. Only Hook remained. Peter leaped forward with his sword.

"You!" screeched Hook as he drew his mighty sword.

"Remember," whispered Wendy to Peter, who was half the size of Hook, "you can do anything if you believe."

Peter nodded and lunged toward Hook. The captain was stronger, but Peter was quicker. He leaped and jabbed, forcing Hook onto the gangplank.

"Stop that infernal ticking," growled Hook. But Peter wasn't ticking. It was the real crocodile, who had seen the commotion and floated out to the ship.

Peter thrust his sword one last time. Hook jumped back, lost his footing, and toppled off the gangplank into the jaws of the crocodile below. The boys cheered.

Wendy smiled. "I knew you could do it," she said. "I believed you could."

The crocodile swam toward shore. His belly chimed two.

"We must leave now to get home before dawn," said Peter. The children flew up into the night, led by Tinker Bell and Peter. In no time they were back at the nursery window.

"Are you sure you want to stay here?" Peter asked Wendy. "You could come back with me to Neverland."

Wendy shook her head. "Neverland was a grand adventure, but this is my home. Would you like to stay here with us?"

Peter gazed at the soft rug and warm beds. He watched Nana nuzzling Michael and licking John's hand. "This is a good place for all of you," he said. "But Neverland is my home."

Wendy nodded. "But you could come back for a visit."

Peter smiled. "Or a story." He bounced on the bed, somersaulted over the nightstand, and flew out the window.

Sometimes, when the night was velvet black and the stars were diamond bright, Wendy would see one star glittering brighter than the rest. She would watch it flit about the night sky, skipping and twirling, and she would sit very still and hear the tiny, silver tinkling above the treetops. She knew fairies were at play. She knew Peter was with them.

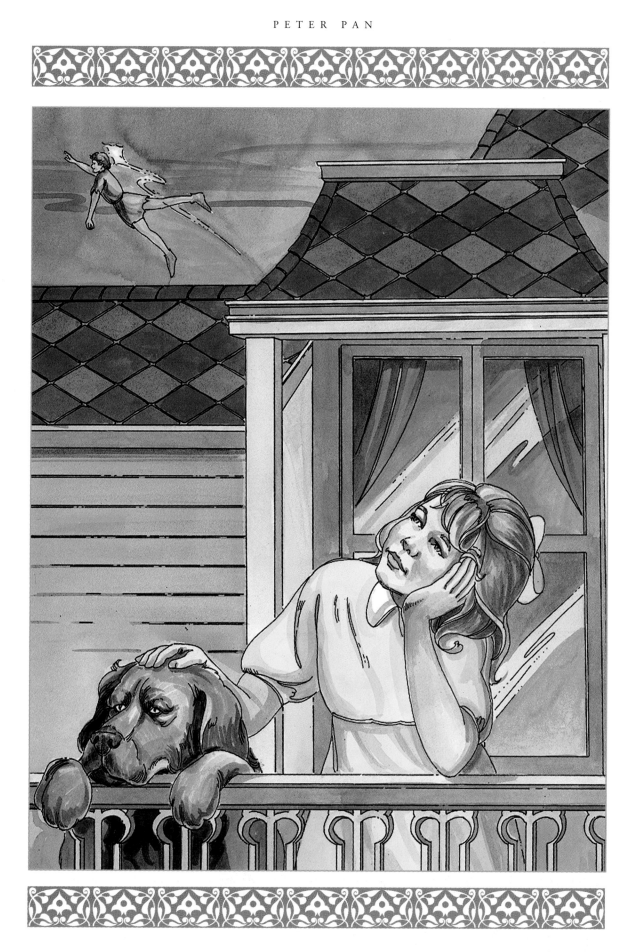

King Midas

Adapted by Jennifer Boudart
Illustrated by Kristen Goeters

There once was a king named Midas, who ruled a magical land of roses and sunshine. King Midas was rich beyond imagination, but he was also very selfish and foolish. King Midas liked to spend his days in the basement of his castle where he kept his gold. Every day he locked himself in the vault so he could count his money without anybody bothering him.

There was nothing that Midas would rather do than count his riches. His gold made him feel important. He loved to surround himself with it. Each morning at the crack of dawn, King Midas headed straight to the vault. He stayed with his gold until he went to sleep at night. And even then he dreamed of how to get more.

King Midas had a beautiful daughter named Marygold. She was very different from her father. Marygold did not pay any attention to gold, and she was not at all selfish. Marygold liked to spend her days outdoors. Day after day Marygold walked happily among the roses in the garden. It was her favorite place. She loved taking care of all the beautiful flowers and watering them so they would grow to be even taller than she was. There was nothing Marygold liked better than smelling the sweet scent of the roses and watching the pretty butterflies as they flew about.

One morning Marygold said to her father, before he went to his vault, "Why don't you join me in the garden today? Come outside to see what a lovely place I've created in the sunshine."

"Oh, no, Marygold," King Midas replied. "I would never enjoy that knowing there is so much gold to count. I really must go down to the vault right away."

King Midas disappeared down the long, winding staircase that led to the basement. This saddened Marygold. She was certain that her father would really enjoy her flowers, especially the roses, if he ever saw them.

Later that day, as Midas was busy counting his gold in the vault, a mysterious stranger appeared. "How did you get in here?" asked King Midas, looking at the locked door.

"Well," said the stranger, "I have some magical powers. My, you certainly have a lot of gold." The stranger gazed around the room at the many stacks and bags of gold.

"Yes," said Midas, "but I could always use more. I like to count a new stack every day."

"I could give you the power to turn all that you touch into gold," said the stranger. "Would you like that?"

Greedy Midas could not believe his ears! "Yes! Yes! Of course I would," Midas excitedly said to the mysterious stranger. "I would like that very much!"

"Very well," said the stranger. "After the next sunrise, anything you touch will turn to gold."

Midas looked around the room with a wide smile. Soon he would have even more money to count! When he looked back to the stranger, he was gone. He had disappeared from the room as mysteriously as he had arrived.

King Midas spent that night wide awake staring through a window in the castle. He could hardly wait for the sun to rise. When the dawn's light finally appeared, Midas reached to push away the curtain, and it turned into solid gold! Then Midas grabbed his chair, and it turned to gold, too! Midas grew very excited with his new magical power. He ran from room to room touching everything he could reach—tables, mirrors, candlesticks, paintings, and doors. Just like the mysterious stranger had promised, everything turned to gold.

"I have the magical touch of gold!" shouted King Midas. "I will be the richest man on earth. No one will ever have as much gold as me."

Then King Midas rushed from his castle and into the morning sunshine. He ran directly into Marygold's garden. He knew that this was his daughter's favorite place. Midas saw many beautiful flowers. He laid his hands on one of the loveliest roses, and it turned from scarlet red to gold. "How delighted Marygold will be," Midas said to himself, "when she finds I have turned all her flowers into precious gold."

Soon the king's stomach began to rumble. Changing things to gold had made him very hungry. Midas returned to the castle and sat down at his table.

"Servant, bring me my breakfast," he ordered. Soon a servant brought plates piled high with the freshest fruit, the warmest bread, and the tastiest cheese. Normally King Midas began eating breakfast with a yummy strawberry. Today he carefully chose the juiciest one. "Ah, look at this bright red strawberry," said King Midas as he reached toward the plate. "Such a delicious beginning to an already wonderful day."

But as soon as he touched it, the strawberry changed to gold. Midas was hungry, but he could not eat. King Midas grabbed a goblet of water and raised it to his lips, but the water turned to gold, too! Midas became dizzy with thirst and hunger. He called to his servants, "Bring me something to eat! I'm so thirsty and hungry!" But everything they brought him turned to gold when he touched it.

Suddenly Marygold came into the room, holding a gold rose. She sat at the table with her father and began to cry.

"Look at this poor rose," Marygold sobbed to her father. "It was the loveliest one in the garden! How could this have happened?"

"I made it happen, Marygold," answered King Midas. "I know that the garden is your favorite place. I thought you would like to see your flowers turned into beautiful and valuable pieces of gold."

"My roses are ruined!" exclaimed Marygold. "They no longer smell sweet, they no longer feel like velvet, and they no longer make the butterflies dance. The roses might be gold, but they are no longer valuable to me. They are worthless!"

Like all fathers, King Midas hated to see his daughter unhappy. He wanted to make Marygold feel better, and without thinking, he rushed over to give her a comforting hug. As soon as King Midas touched her, Marygold turned into solid gold!

King Midas was shocked at what he had done to Marygold. He quickly ran from the golden statue. He now knew his wish to turn all that he touched to gold had been a curse, not a blessing. If only he could turn back time, then he could get his beautiful daughter back.

King Midas sat down on the floor. How could he have been so greedy? He picked up the golden rose that Marygold had dropped. He began to cry.

Just then the mysterious stranger returned and asked, "Aren't you pleased with all your gold?"

"I was very foolish," King Midas answered. "I don't care about gold anymore. I just want Marygold again. Please save her, and you can have all my gold."

"I do not want your gold, Midas. I just wanted to teach you a lesson. To get your daughter back, simply go to the river beyond the rose garden. Dive into its waters and bring back enough water to sprinkle over the things you have turned to gold. They will all return to normal."

At once King Midas called out to all the servants in the castle. "Gather every pail, bucket, bowl, and pitcher you can find," he shouted. "Then follow me to the river beyond the rose garden! I need your help to change Marygold and all the flowers back to normal." Without another word Midas and the servants ran to the river's edge.

Midas leaped into the cold, rushing water of the river, and it instantly began to turn golden yellow. He and his servants quickly filled their pails and bowls before the water completely changed.

King Midas ran straight to the dining hall, and splashed water over every golden object, just like the mysterious stranger had told him to do. When Midas saw Marygold change from gold back to her normal self, his heart filled with joy.

King Midas was very thankful to have his daughter back. Together he and Marygold went outside and changed all the gold flowers back to beautiful red roses. The mysterious stranger had taught Midas a valuable lesson: there are more important things in life than gold.

From that day on, King Midas was happier than he had ever been before. He no longer spent his days locked away in the vault. Instead he shared time with Marygold in the garden. Now Midas cared little for gold and riches. He saw the true beauty of flowers, butterflies, and his most valuable treasure, Marygold.

The only gold that King Midas cared for now was the golden sunshine.

The Sleeping Beauty

Adapted by Jane Jerrard
Illustrated by Burgandy Nilles

Once upon a time in a far-off land, there lived a good king and queen who wanted a child more than anything in the world. After many wishful years, the queen at last gave birth to a little daughter, and the whole land joined in the parents' happiness.

The king invited all the people in the kingdom to a great party to celebrate the birth of the princess. The queen asked seven fairies to be the baby girl's godmothers. The fairies were all invited to the party.

When the day of the celebration arrived, the fairy godmothers were the first guests to enter the castle.

The palace servants escorted the seven fairy godmothers into the dining hall. The fairies sat down at a fine table at the head of the room. Each fairy had a place setting with golden plates and cups decorated with diamonds and rubies.

But there was another fairy—a very old and unhappy fairy—whom the queen had forgotten to invite. As the guests sat down, this fairy appeared among them. She was very angry at having been forgotten, so the queen apologized and quickly ordered another place set for her among the other fairies. But there were no more golden plates or jeweled cups. The old fairy had to eat off a china plate and sip from a crystal glass. This made her even angrier than before.

As dinner was served, the fairies talked excitedly among themselves about their gifts for the princess. But the evil old fairy did not join in their conversations. She only grumbled to herself. The beautiful young fairy who sat beside her at the fine table heard the evil old woman muttering to herself during dinner. The young fairy decided to hide behind the curtains in case the old fairy caused some mischief.

After the feast was completed, many of the guests presented the princess with wonderful gifts. She received beautiful handmade dresses, jeweled combs for her hair, and wonderful books to read when she grew older. The king and queen thanked their subjects for each wonderful gift.

Finally the time came for the godmothers to give their gifts. While the king and queen sat proudly nearby, each fairy in turn stepped up to the cradle where the baby princess slept. Each fairy gave the child a magical gift.

"I give this child beauty," said the first fairy godmother.

"She shall be as good as she is lovely," said the second fairy godmother.

"She shall have happiness all her days," offered the third. The princess was also given gifts of a quick mind, dancing feet, and a beautiful voice.

Then the old fairy stepped forward. She was angry at having been forgotten by the queen. "I give this princess a curse. On her sixteenth birthday she will prick her finger on the spindle of a spinning wheel and die."

The king and queen, their guests, and the other six fairies shook with fear at the evil fairy's terrible curse. "What shall we do?" cried the queen.

Then the seventh fairy quietly stepped out from her hiding place behind the curtain. She was the youngest of all the fairy godmothers and the kindest. But her magical powers were not yet as strong as those of the other fairies. She could not reverse the evil fairy's curse.

"I do not have the power to take away this curse," she said sadly, "but I can change it. The princess will not die when the spindle pricks her finger. Instead she will fall into a deep sleep that will last for a hundred years. Our princess will awaken when she receives the kiss of a king's son."

The king and queen thanked the young fairy, but they were stricken by grief and found little comfort in her gift. In the years before her sixteenth birthday, they did everything they could to prevent the curse from being fulfilled. The king ordered all the spinning wheels in his kingdom destroyed to try to save his little daughter.

As the years went by, the princess grew into a beautiful girl, blessed with all her fairy godmothers' gifts. It had been so long since the royal banquet that many people in the kingdom forgot about the evil fairy's curse. Even the king and queen forgot about it, since all the kingdom's spinning wheels had been destroyed years ago.

Finally the day of the princess's sixteenth birthday arrived. That morning she decided to explore some of the towers in the castle where she had never been. At the top of the tallest tower, she came upon a little room where an old woman sat at a spinning wheel. The princess had never seen a spinning wheel since they had not been allowed in the kingdom in her lifetime. The princess asked the old woman what she was doing.

"I am spinning, my dear," replied the woman.

"How clever!" said the girl. "Please let me try."

The old woman eagerly got up from the stool, and helped the princess sit down. But as soon as the princess started to spin, she pricked her finger on the spindle. Immediately she fell into a deep, deep sleep.

No one in the kingdom could wake the sleeping beauty. With great sadness in their hearts, the king and queen dressed her in a fine white gown and laid her in her royal bed. They surrounded her with silk pillows and soft blankets and brought her fresh flowers every day.

When the seventh fairy heard that the curse had come to pass, she flew to the kingdom. She knew that the princess would be frightened to wake up among strangers, and she knew that the king and queen would be very sad to watch their daughter sleep through the rest of their days.

The little fairy decided to cast a magical spell over the whole kingdom. She touched all the people in the kingdom with her magic wand. The fairy touched all the servants in the castle and the king and queen. She even touched the princess's little dog. Everyone the fairy touched fell fast asleep and would not awaken until the princess opened her eyes.

Last of all she grew a magical forest of thorny trees around the castle to protect it. Then everything in the kingdom was still for a hundred years.

As the years passed the people in the surrounding countryside forgot the kingdom hidden in the thorny woods. A few of the older people remembered the story of the sleeping beauty, but eventually her tale faded from memory.

Then one day a young prince was out riding over the hills, exploring the countryside. He came upon the dark, thorny woods and wondered why it was so silent. Finally he noticed a tower rising above the trees.

"What is that castle I see in the woods?" he asked some people who were passing along the road.

But no one knew. The prince rode into a village nearby and asked about the strange castle. Finally a very old man told the prince a tale that his father had told him about the hidden castle. It was the story of the sleeping beauty.

The prince grew very excited upon hearing this tale and decided to rescue the beautiful princess. He drew his sword and prepared to cut his way through the thorny forest to reach her, but the trees parted magically to make a path for him—a path right to the castle door!

The prince entered the silent castle. Everywhere he looked, he saw people sleeping soundly. Cooks snored loudly in the kitchen, maids slept upon their brooms, and the king dreamed on his throne.

The prince searched through the entire enchanted castle before he found the princess, lying in her bed of gold and silver. At the sight of her, he leaned down and kissed her cheek.

The princess opened her eyes. When she saw the handsome young man, she smiled and asked, "Is it you, my prince?"

The prince was charmed at the sound of her voice and told her that, indeed, he had come to save her. Then he told her that he loved her already for he had dreamed of this meeting.

The prince and princess were interrupted by a great cheer. The whole castle was awake! The king and queen thanked the young prince for breaking the spell. The king called for a great celebration which lasted for many days and many nights, since they were not sleepy at all!

At the end of the party, the princess and prince were married in the palace, and their life together was happier than they had ever dreamed possible.

The Elves and the Shoemaker

Adapted by Jennifer Boudart
Illustrated by Kristen Goeters

There once was a shoemaker who lived with his wife. He enjoyed his work very much and set up his shop inside their small house. Times were hard for the shoemaker and his wife. Snowstorms had kept everyone indoors for weeks, so no one could buy any shoes. The shoemaker had little money for food, and he had only enough leather left to make one more pair of shoes. His wife asked, "What are we to do? The cupboards are bare, and we have no firewood. Even our last candle has almost burned away." Her voice was gentle. She knew her husband worked hard for what little they had.

The shoemaker looked lovingly at his wife. "We must not worry," he said. "Things will work out for us. You'll see, I will finish these shoes tomorrow, and someone will buy them." He cut out the leather and then went to bed. The shoemaker would finish working first thing in the morning.

When the shoemaker woke up early the next morning, the whole house was cold. His body shivered, and he was very tired. The shoemaker went to his workbench, rubbing his tired eyes. When he looked down, the shoemaker thought he would find the pieces of leather just as he had left them. What he saw instead made him rub his eyes again. A finished pair of shoes were on the workbench!

The shoemaker ran his hands over the shoes. Sure enough, they were made from the very same leather that he had cut the previous night. The shoes were very beautiful! The shoemaker admired the tight, even stitching, the placement of the bows, and the silky shine of the leather. He could not have made better shoes himself. The shoemaker called to his wife. She was just as amazed as he was. "Who could have made these shoes?" she asked.

The shoemaker and his wife did not know who had given them such a wonderful gift. They did know that the shoes were worth a lot and would bring a good price.

"What a great day," said the shoemaker. "We have a pair of shoes to sell, and the weather is finally clear. Maybe our good luck will continue and someone will buy these shoes."

At that moment there was a knock on the shop door. It was a traveler who had seen the shoemaker's sign. "I work for the king," he explained. "I have been traveling throughout the countryside. My travels have worn holes in my shoes. I was hoping that I could buy a pair from you."

"You've come on the right day," answered the shoemaker. "I have a pair of fine shoes right here." The shoemaker showed the beautiful shoes to the traveler.

"Those are indeed lovely," he said. "And you are an excellent craftsman." The traveler tried on the new shoes. They fit his feet perfectly. He walked around the shop for a few moments and said, "These are the most comfortable shoes I've ever worn." Then he gave the shoemaker a shiny gold coin to pay for them.

With the gold coin the shoemaker had enough money to buy some things he really needed. He bought food, firewood, and enough leather to make two pairs of shoes. He also bought a wool shawl for his wife.

The couple was very thankful for their good luck, and they decided they would work harder than ever to keep it. Once again the shoemaker cut the leather into pieces ready for sewing and placed them on his workbench. The next morning he found two more pairs of finished shoes. And they were just as good as the first pair!

Within hours the shoemaker sold both pairs of shoes and bought more leather. The next day there were four pairs of shoes waiting on the workbench. This continued for many nights, until the shoemaker's shelves were filled with beautiful shoes like no one had ever seen before.

Life soon changed for the shoemaker. Now he and his wife always had wood for the fire and food to eat. The shoemaker bought better tools, lots of leather, and the best brass buckles. He bought his wife an oil lamp, a new blanket, and a lace cap.

The shoemaker was always kind to the people who traveled from all over the kingdom to buy his shoes. He could have charged high prices, but instead he charged just enough to live a comfortable life.

Word of the shoemaker's fine shoes soon made him the most popular shoemaker in the land. But still something bothered the shoemaker. One evening he said to his wife, "Every night, while we are tucked in our beds, someone is working hard to help us. It's a shame we don't even know who it is. Why don't we stay up to find out?"

That night the shoemaker cut the leather into pieces and placed them on his workbench. Just like always, he turned down the oil lamp and left the room. But instead of going to bed, he and his wife hid in the doorway.

The moon rose and filled the room with silver light. Soon something was moving on the workbench. Two elves were there! They stood just a few inches tall, no taller than the shoe they were sewing. The elves began to work, helping each other handle the leather and tools.

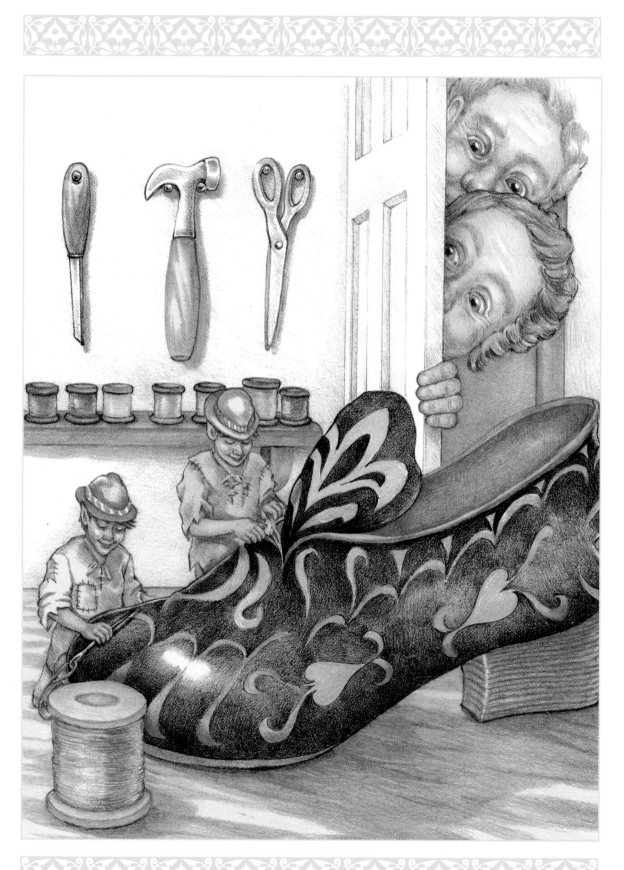

The clothing of the elves was old and worn, which made the shoemaker and his wife sad. The elves wore thin, torn pants and shirts that were ripped and covered with patches. They were making shoes, but they didn't have any for themselves. They must have been cold, but their cheery faces and busy hands didn't show it. The couple tiptoed off to bed, leaving the elves to do their work.

The next morning the shoemaker and his wife looked at the newly made shoes that were on the workbench, and they thought about the elves. "Did you see how quickly those little fellows worked together and how carefully they placed each stitch?" asked the shoemaker.

His wife frowned and said, "I only saw their poor clothing and bare feet. Clearly they are in great need."

Her husband agreed and said, "I have an idea! We will make those little elves the clothes they need! They are so tiny that it will be easy for me to make some fine shoes for them."

His wife clapped her hands. "Yes! And I will use a bit of my wool shawl and a corner from our blanket to make proper pants and coats."

The shoemaker and his wife made two tiny suits of clothing and two pairs of shoes. That evening, instead of leaving pieces of leather on the bench, they left the clothes and shoes. Once again they hid behind the doorway and waited for the elves to come.

The elves magically appeared at midnight. They climbed upon the workbench then stopped in their tracks.

"What is this?" asked one in a little voice.

"Where are the pieces of leather and the tools?" asked the other.

Suddenly both elves saw the two tiny suits. Their little faces brightened and they shouted gleefully. At once they put on the fine new suits and shoes. They were so excited they began to dance and sing:

> *What merry little elves are we!*
>
> *These fine clothes fit us perfectly!*
>
> *Who'd be so kind? We wish we knew!*
>
> *We'd like to give our thanks to you!*

The shoemaker and his wife were so pleased they could hardly keep themselves from cheering!

Weeks passed, and the shoemaker's shop was always filled with people. He still offered the finest shoes in the land, and people from all around wanted a pair. Even the king had bought twenty of his loveliest shoes. With the great success of their shop, the shoemaker and his wife lived very comfortably.

One thing had changed, though. The elves had not come back since the night they received their new suits of clothes and shoes. The shoemaker and his wife did not mind.

"Ah, wife," said the shoemaker, "I enjoy my work and am happy to be back at this workbench. We should be grateful to those elves."

"That is true, dear," answered his wife. "The elves worked so hard for us and were so nice to us. I'm just glad we were able to help them in return."

In the evenings, while the shoemaker cut leather at his bench and his wife baked bread, they thought about the two elves. Because of their kindness and hard work, the shoemaker and his wife lived happily. Their cupboards were always filled, and their house was always warm.

Beauty and the Beast

Adapted by Jane Jerrard
Illustrated by Burgandy Nilles

There once was a rich man who had six children—three daughters and three sons. After a lifetime of good luck, the man suddenly fell upon hard times. His house burned down and his ships sank at sea.

He and his children were forced to move into a small cottage in the country, where they lived on food that they grew themselves. His two oldest daughters were very unhappy. They were sure that no young gentlemen would want to marry them now that they were poor. But the youngest, named Beauty, was always hopeful. She tried to make their new life as comfortable as possible.

One day the man heard that one of his ships had sailed safely into harbor. He decided to go to the port to see this for himself, even though it was a long ride. His other children asked their father to bring back expensive presents for them, but Beauty asked only for her father's safe return.

"Isn't there anything at all that I can bring you, Beauty?" asked her father.

"If you see one, I would like to have a rose," she said, for Beauty missed the beautiful gardens of their old home.

Beauty's father reached the port safely, only to find that his ship had been robbed and that he was now poorer than before. Making his way back home through a thick forest, the unlucky man was lost in a terrible snowstorm. It was so cold that the man was sure he would perish in the night.

Suddenly, up ahead, he saw a row of flowering trees and at the same time felt warm air on his face! He walked a little farther to find himself in the middle of a beautiful, summery garden. The snow instantly melted away from his coat and the warmth returned to his numb fingers and toes.

The father had stumbled upon an enchanted castle. He explored the gardens, where no snow had fallen, then went to the great front door of the castle. No one answered his knock, so the man pushed the door open and went inside.

He walked through the castle's great hallway, which was as silent as a churchyard. He found a cheerful little room with a table of hot food waiting for him. He ate hungrily then fell asleep in front of the fire.

The next morning there was still no sign of anyone in the castle, so the man decided to depart for home. On his way through the gardens, he saw a rosebush blooming with beautiful red roses. He remembered Beauty's request and selected one of the flowers for his daughter.

Just as the man snipped the flower from its branch, a horrible beast in a fine suit appeared as if by magic! "Is this how you thank me? I feed and shelter you and then you steal from me?" growled the beast.

The man begged for his life, explaining that the rose was a gift for one of his daughters.

The beast said that he would not kill the man but would accept one of his daughters instead. He promised to treat the daughter kindly if she would come to live with him.

"Please," begged the father. "Take me instead!"

But the beast refused.

The man returned home that day and told his children what had happened. Neither of the two oldest daughters wanted to go to live with the beast.

"It's all right, Father," Beauty said quietly. "It was my rose that started the trouble, and so I must be the one to go."

The other children all agreed that Beauty should go. Their father was sad, for Beauty was his favorite daughter. He also knew that she was the bravest. The very next day, Beauty rode away with her father.

Again they found no one in the enchanted castle, and again supper was set on the table. This time the beast appeared as they finished eating. Beauty was frightened by the beast's terrible face, but he spoke to her gently, asking if she would stay with him to save her father's life.

Beauty told the beast she would stay. So her father left her there, although it broke his heart, and she made the beast's castle her home. Beauty had her own big room with mirrors for walls and a clock that woke her by calling out her name. She spent her days alone, exploring the wonders of the enchanted castle.

Every night she sat down to dinner with the beast. He was quite fierce-looking, but his voice was quiet and gentle, and he always spoke kindly to Beauty. Soon she was no longer afraid of him and found herself growing more and more fond of him.

In fact Beauty came to look forward to their quiet evenings together.

After dinner they would walk through the beautiful gardens and talk of many things. No matter what they discussed, the beast would ask Beauty the same question every night.

"Am I very ugly?" he asked her.

"Yes, you are," she would always answer, "but I like you anyway."

"Then will you marry me, Beauty?" he would ask.

"Oh, please do not ask me this question," she would say to the beast and turn away.

Beauty was happy in the magical castle, and she had grown very fond of the beast. But she missed her own home, her brothers and sisters, and her loving father.

One night in the garden she asked the beast to let her go home for a visit.

"You may visit your family," said the beast, "but you must promise to return here in two months." Beauty thanked the beast and kissed him on his furry cheek. The beast only looked at her with a little sadness in his eyes. He had grown to love Beauty and would miss her more than she knew.

The beast gave Beauty two magic trunks to fill with presents from the enchanted castle for her family. "How delighted my sisters will be," thought Beauty. No matter how much she packed, the trunks were never full.

When Beauty was ready to go home, the beast gave her a special gift. It was a magic ring with a large red jewel. The beast told her the ring would take her home and then bring her back. All she had to do was turn it on her finger, and she would be back at the enchanted castle that very instant!

The next morning Beauty awoke to the sound of her father's voice! She was home in her own bed. Her family was very happy to see her. Her father's luck had finally returned, and his family was rich once more.

Beauty's family made a wonderful feast that night to welcome her home. Everyone gathered around the table and listened while Beauty told them of the enchanted castle and of her kind friend, the beast. Later, as Beauty pulled gift after gift from the magical trunks, her family marvelled at the beast's generosity.

Beauty was very happy to see her family again. But as the weeks passed, she missed the enchanted castle where she had been so happy. She missed the wonderful food and beautiful flowers that always seemed to appear magically on her table. But most of all she missed the beast. She spent hours thinking of their long talks at dinnertime, and she fondly remembered their evening strolls through the gardens.

Beauty found that she was growing restless among her family, but she was afraid to tell them that she wanted to leave. She did not want to break her father's heart again.

One night Beauty missed the beast more than usual. She took the magic ring out of her jewelry box and put it on her finger. When she looked deep into the jewel, she saw the beast lying in his garden. He seemed to be dying!

"Oh, my poor, wonderful beast!" cried Beauty.

With that she turned the ring on her finger and was magically returned to the enchanted garden. Beauty gasped when she saw the beast lying on the ground. He seemed nearly dead. Beauty rushed to his side, but the beast was so weak he could not say a word. She lifted his head, and he opened his eyes to look at her one last time.

"Oh, please do not die!" cried Beauty. "I never knew it before, but I love you!"

At Beauty's words there was a sudden flash of light, and the beast leaped up. Beauty saw that her ugly friend had changed into a handsome prince! Beauty's true love had freed the prince from the spell of an evil enchantress. Since the two already loved each other, they were married and lived happily ever after in the enchanted castle.

Stone Soup

Adapted by Mary Rowitz
Illustrated by Sharron O'Neil

A hungry traveler had been roaming the countryside for a long time, and he hadn't eaten a good meal in quite a while. One day the traveler spotted a lovely village off in the distance. The hungry traveler became very excited and said to himself, "I'm bound to find someone in the village who will share a meal with me."

As the traveler hurried to the town, he tripped over a stone in the road. The stone was not like any that the traveler had ever seen. It was perfectly smooth and oval in shape. The traveler looked at the stone carefully and decided he would keep it. "You never know when a stone like this might come in handy," he said.

Then the traveler happily headed to the village.

When the traveler arrived in the village, things did not go as well as he had hoped. He stopped at a few houses with no luck finding a meal. No one had any food to share. One house the traveler came to was very quiet. All the doors and windows were closed, and the shades were drawn. The traveler began to think that no one was home. Finally a maid appeared in the doorway. "Can you spare some food?" the traveler asked her. "I have been traveling for days and am very hungry."

"I'm sorry, but I have only a few potatoes," the maid said. "There's not enough to spare or share. Why don't you try my neighbor next door?"

"I already have," said the traveler, "but he was very grumpy and just slammed the door. It looks like finding some food in this village will be more difficult than I thought."

"I'm sorry, but I cannot help you," said the maid as she closed the door.

The hungry traveler refused to give up. He walked through the village, knocking on doors.

The traveler visited every house in the village, but no one had enough food to spare or share.

"I only have some carrots," said one villager.

"I only have this cabbage," said another.

"I don't have any food," said a third. "I only have a little salt and pepper!"

Since there was no food for the hungry traveler, he decided to move on. He followed the path that lead out of the village. His stomach grumbled and turned as he walked. Before he got very far, the traveler began to feel tired. He decided to get some rest in the cool shade of a tree just outside the village. As he sat under the tree, the traveler looked back at the quiet little town. "It's a shame," he thought, "such a nice village and such a beautiful day, but nobody is outdoors talking or playing."

Then the traveler reached into his bag and took out the smooth, oval stone he had found earlier in the day. Such a curious stone, he thought. Surely it must be special. As he sat admiring the stone, the traveler suddenly had a brilliant idea!

The traveler ran back to the village and shouted, "Come out of your houses, everybody! I have a magic stone! It will give us enough food for a wonderful meal. Everyone in town will have plenty to eat, and there will even be enough to spare and share!"

One by one, the curious villagers peeked out of their doors and windows.

The grumpy villager who slammed the door on the traveler earlier that day looked out his window and shouted, "What's all the racket about?"

"Come help me make a pot of delicious stone soup," said the traveler.

The maid stepped out of her house. "Stone soup? I've never heard of stone soup before," she said.

Two excited children ran up to the traveler. "Is that your tummy growling?" one child asked.

"Yes," replied the other.

"Soon your stomachs will no longer grumble," said the hungry traveler. "We will all have our fill of delicious stone soup!"

"Does anybody have a large soup kettle to get us started?" the traveler asked. The villagers looked at each other without saying a word. Finally the big, grumpy villager broke the silence.

"I've got a black kettle that you can use," he said, "but I don't think it will do any good. I don't think there is such a thing as stone soup. Who ever heard of a magic stone?"

Most of the villagers were excited, but some felt the same way as the big, grumpy villager. "Do you really believe he can make soup from a stone?" asked one young lady.

"I guess we'll find out soon," said another. "I certainly hope he can. I haven't had good soup in a long time."

The grumpy villager brought out his large kettle and placed it on a pile of sticks for the fire. "Here you go," he said. "Now let's see if that magic stone of yours can really make enough soup for all of us."

"Don't worry," said the traveler. "There will be plenty."

The villagers gathered around the pot to see what the traveler would do next.

The traveler placed the smooth, oval stone into the kettle of water and began to stir. After a little while he tasted the soup. "Not bad," he said, "but I think it could use salt and pepper."

"I've got some," said one of the young ladies. "I'll run home and get it."

"Perhaps the soup would taste even better if I shared a few of my potatoes," the maid suggested.

"Yes, that's a great idea," said the traveler. "Why don't you get them, and we'll add them right away."

The young lady returned and sprinkled her salt and pepper into the kettle. Then the maid came back and dropped in her potatoes. Once again the traveler stirred the stone soup. When he tasted it for the second time, all the villagers watched him with anticipation.

"This is very good, but it would taste even better with some carrots and cabbage," said the traveler. Then a young boy ran home to get some carrots, and a little girl ran home to get her cabbage. The traveler smiled wide with each new addition.

By now everyone was having so much fun that they forgot how hungry they were. Even the big, grumpy villager was no longer grumpy. "Let's make this meal a party!" he shouted.

"Just think," said the little boy, "a huge kettle of soup made from a magic stone. I can't wait to try it!"

"Neither can I," said the girl.

Finally the traveler announced that the stone soup was ready to eat. He filled all the bowls, and the villagers began to eat. Afterward there was plenty of soup left over. "There's enough to spare and share!" said the young lady.

The villagers were so happy after dinner that they didn't want the evening to end. They started playing music and dancing.

"I didn't know you could play the banjo," the maid said to the big villager.

"And I didn't know you could play the washboard," he responded.

"I think there was a lot we didn't know until the traveler came along," said the maid.

The villagers shared a wonderful evening together. They played music and danced late into the night. At last the village was alive with chatter and laughter.

The next morning the traveler said good-bye to his new friends. It was time for him to leave. "I want you to have this," the traveler said as he handed the smooth, oval stone to one of the villagers. "Now you will always be able to make stone soup together, and you will never be hungry or sad or grumpy again." Each of the villagers hugged the traveler and told him to come back and visit some time. They were all very grateful and hoped to see the traveler again.

The traveler followed the road that led out of the lovely little village. As the traveler walked along his way, he stumbled over another stone in the road. He picked it up at once and admired its dark, jagged edges. The traveler looked at the stone carefully and finally decided to keep it. "You never know when a special stone like this might come in handy," he said to himself as he placed it in his bag.

Jack and the Beanstalk

Adapted by Sarah Toast
Illustrated by Susan Spellman

A poor woman lived alone in the country with her son, Jack. Years ago, when Jack was just a baby, a terrible giant had done away with Jack's father and stolen his gold and treasure.

Jack and his mother both worked hard. But no matter how hard they tried, there never seemed to be enough money to buy food. At last there was no money at all. Jack's mother said, "Jack, dear, take the cow to market today, and sell her for a good price."

On his way to market, Jack met a stranger who showed him five magic beans.

The man asked Jack where he was going. Jack replied, "I'm going to market to sell this cow, so my mother and I can have food to eat."

"I will give you these five magic beans for the cow," said the stranger. Jack thought that was a good deal, so he traded the cow for the beans.

When Jack returned to the cottage, he burst through the door and said, "Look at the five magic beans I got for the cow!"

"Jack, what have you done? Those beans aren't worth anything! Now we will go hungry," cried his mother as she threw the beans out the window. Jack and his mother quietly went to bed without any supper.

Jack woke up early the next morning and went outside. He was amazed to see a huge beanstalk had sprung up outside the window during the night. It had grown so high that he couldn't see the top. Jack decided to see where it led.

Jack climbed the beanstalk for a very long time. When he finally reached the top, he saw a great castle.

Tired and hungry after his long climb, Jack began walking through the clouds toward the mighty castle. Maybe someone at the castle could give him something to eat and a little work to do, thought Jack.

When he reached the castle steps, Jack couldn't believe his eyes! At the door stood a woman ten times larger than anyone he had ever seen. "Please, ma'am," said Jack, "I haven't eaten for a very long time. Could you give me supper?"

"If you stay here, you'll be the giant's supper," the woman said. Jack was scared. He realized that this was the wife of the giant— the same giant who had killed his father. Jack was so hungry, he still begged for something to eat. The woman finally gave in and let Jack come into the kitchen. She fixed a plate of food and gave it to him.

Jack had just finished eating when he heard the thump, thump, thump of heavy footsteps. Jack was so frightened, he couldn't move. Just as the giant came into the kitchen, the woman popped Jack into the cool oven to hide him.

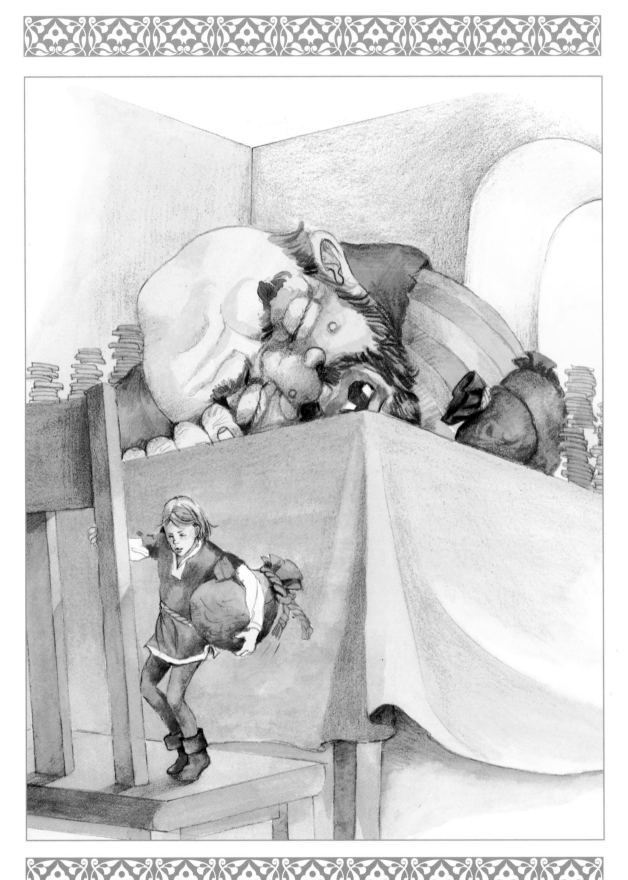

When the giant arrived, he sniffed the air and roared:

Fee-fi-fo-fum!

I smell the blood of an Englishman!

"It's just your supper that you smell," said the giant's wife.

The giant gobbled up his entire supper. Jack watched from his hiding place. He had never seen anyone eat so much food. Then the giant said to his wife, "Bring me my gold!"

The woman brought out the gold. Jack kept very still as he watched the giant count the gold over and over. Finally the giant fell asleep. Jack's mother once told him that his father's gold had been stolen by the mean giant. Jack quietly climbed up on the table. He was a little scared to be so near the giant, but he knew what he had to do. Jack snatched a bag of gold and ran away.

Jack ran out the castle door and through the clouds. When he reached the beanstalk, he dropped the gold down to his mother's garden and then climbed down as fast as he could.

Jack's mother was very happy when the gold coins rained down and Jack came back safely. At last they would have food on their table! That night they had a big meal with food from the market.

The mother and son made the gold last for a very long time, but finally there was no more. Jack decided to climb the beanstalk again. He would have to get back all of his father's treasure despite any danger.

Jack returned to the giant's castle. He crept softly into the kitchen and hid in the oven again. Soon the giant's footsteps shook the floor, and he roared:

Fee-fi-fo-fum!

I smell the blood of an Englishman!

"There's no one here," said the giant's wife. The giant ate his supper quickly, then bellowed for his hen.

Then the giant shouted, "Lay!" Jack peeked out and saw the hen lay a perfect golden egg. After the giant fell asleep, Jack jumped out of the oven, grabbed the hen, and ran away.

When Jack reached the beanstalk, he scaled down quickly while carrying the hen. His mother was happy to see him return home safely. When she saw the hen, Jack's mother told him that it had once belonged to his father. "Now there is only one treasure still missing," added Jack's mother, "a magic harp."

The hen laid a golden egg every time it was told to lay, so Jack and his mother now had everything they needed. After awhile, however, Jack thought about the harp that used to belong to his father. Even though he would face great danger, Jack decided to climb the beanstalk one last time. He would make his way to the castle and find the harp.

As soon as he arrived at the castle, Jack sneaked into the kitchen and hid in a huge copper pot. The giant thumped into the kitchen at suppertime, sniffing the air:

Fee-fi-fo-fum!
I smell the blood of an Englishman!

This time the giant's wife ran to the oven and looked inside, but it was empty.

The giant looked all around the kitchen, peering into tea pots and under the chairs. Jack was terribly afraid of being found. Luckily the giant never checked inside the big copper pot that held Jack!

The hungry giant sat down for his supper. He gobbled up his food and then called for his wife to bring his harp. She scurried from the room and quickly returned with a very special harp made of gold. The giant commanded the harp to play. Its golden strings filled the kitchen with beautiful music. Then the harp began to sing a slow lullaby. It was the loveliest voice that Jack had ever heard.

Soon the giant fell asleep. As he began snoring loudly, his wife left the room. When Jack knew the moment was right, he climbed out of the pot and onto the table. The giant's mighty snore roared into Jack's ears. He took a deep breath, grabbed the harp, and started to run off with it.

With the harp in his arms, Jack jumped off the table and ran for his life. But before he had left the castle, the harp began to cry, "Master! Master!" The giant awoke with a start at the sound of the golden cries.

Jumping from his chair, he chased Jack out the castle door and through the clouds. Jack could hear the giant's thunderous steps crashing down right behind him. Although the giant took very big footsteps, he was unable to catch Jack. He had eaten such a huge supper that he was unable to move very quickly. Jack reached the beanstalk first.

Jack hurried down the beanstalk with the harp. He called to his mother as he went, "Mother! Bring me the ax!"

The giant was already halfway down the beanstalk when Jack reached the ground. Jack quickly took the ax from his mother and with one mighty chop, he cut down the beanstalk. The giant crashed down to the ground, and that was the end of him!

Brave Jack and his mother lived happily ever after and never went hungry again.

The Emperor's New Clothes

Adapted by Mary Rowitz
Illustrated by Sherry Neidigh

Once upon a time there was an emperor who loved clothes more than anything else. He had more clothes than anyone in the land. The emperor's clothes filled all the closets and most of the rooms in the royal palace.

It was a good thing the emperor was very rich because he spent so much money on clothes. The emperor selected only the finest, most comfortable fabrics, and he hired the most skilled tailors.

The emperor also spent a lot of money on mirrors. He thought his fancy clothes made him look quite dashing, so he spent most of his free time looking at himself.

The emperor's pride was well known throughout the kingdom. Everyone thought he was quite silly to spend so much time in front of his mirrors. They made jokes behind the emperor's back, but no one ever said anything directly to his face. They did not want to make the emperor angry because he was, after all, the ruler of the land.

Word of the silly emperor who loved fine clothes reached two thieves in a faraway land. Instead of making jokes about him, the thieves thought of a plan. "We can use the emperor's pride to make ourselves rich," said one thief.

"The emperor will never even know that he's been cheated." laughed the other.

The thieves dressed up as traveling tailors and made the long journey to the emperor's palace. When they arrived at the palace gate, they told the guards that they had special fabrics to show the emperor. They pretended to have the rarest and most wonderful fabrics in all the world. The emperor should see them at once. Of course, the guards let them pass through the gate. The two thieves were taken directly to the throne room.

The sneaky thieves presented themselves to the emperor and his wife. They explained that their fabric was not only wonderful, but magical, too. "Only the wisest people in the land will see this fabric," they said. "It will be invisible to fools and to those who are unfit for their office."

The thieves opened their bag. They appeared to carefully lift something into the air. They held their arms before the emperor and his wife.

The emperor squinted. He saw nothing at all in their hands! "Why, I must be a fool," he thought. "Either that or I do not deserve to sit on this throne!" The emperor was embarrassed that he could not see the fabric, so he said, "That is simply the most magnificent fabric I have ever seen."

The emperor asked his wife what she thought of the magical fabric. She squinted, too. She couldn't see anything, but she did not want anyone to think she was a fool, so she said, "It is quite extraordinary. It's like no other fabric that I know."

The two thieves nodded in agreement.

Knowing his wife was no fool, the emperor thought the fabric must be real, even though he could not see it. "I will offer you twenty pieces of gold to make me a new suit with this magical fabric," said the emperor.

The thieves were delighted. They thanked the emperor and went to work right away. They requested permission to measure the emperor for the special suit.

"When you wear this suit, it will feel as light as a spider's web against your skin," one thief said as he measured the top of the emperor's head. "It will even feel as gentle as a breeze in the warm summertime."

The other thief then added, "You might even feel as though you're wearing nothing at all."

"I can't wait to wear my new suit," said the emperor excitedly. "It really sounds like the most wonderful fabric! No one else in all the world will have a suit as magnificent as mine. Please work quickly. I want my suit as soon as possible."

The thieves smiled slyly and winked at each other behind the emperor's back. They had finished sizing him up.

After a few days, the royal minister went to see how the new suit was coming along. He wanted to make sure the tailors were working as fast as possible. The emperor became more anxious for his new suit with each passing day. The minister was stunned by what he didn't see. The tailors were cutting away at the air with their scissors, and stitching up fabric that wasn't there! "Could it be that I am a fool?" the minister gulped.

Seeing the minister, one of the thieves said, "Please tell the emperor that his suit will be ready soon. Don't you think this material is beautiful?" The thief held out his arms and pretended to admire the fabric.

"Oh, yes," said the minister, nodding his head. He didn't want to look like a fool.

"But first," said the thief, "please order another tray of food for us. All this hard work is making us very hungry."

That much must be true, the minister thought as he saw apple cores, chicken legs, and bits of cheese all over the floor. The thieves had eaten so much already. They must be working hard on something!

Finally the thieves brought the emperor his new suit. They stretched their arms out before him and said, "Behold, sir, the most magnificent suit in all the land!"

The king gasped. Truly the suit must be beautiful, he thought, even though he couldn't see it at all. He put the suit on slowly, being careful not to snag the fine stitching that the tailors described. Then he strutted around the room. He had never felt so dashing.

"This is truly the finest suit I have ever had," the emperor said to the royal minister. "Tell me, what do you think of it?"

"If you are happy, then I am happy," said the royal minister with a nod. But the minister was anything but happy. In his eyes the emperor was standing in front of a mirror in his underwear, admiring a new suit that wasn't even there!

The emperor wanted to show off his new suit to everyone in the land. He asked the royal minister to call for a royal parade the next day.

"If that is what you want," said the minister, "then you shall have your parade."

Everyone in the kingdom was excited about the parade. They had long grown bored with stories of the emperor's clothes, but what interested them now was the new, magical fabric. They had all heard that fools could not see it, and they wanted to find out who among them was a fool.

On the day of the parade, everyone pushed and shoved to get the best view. At the sound of the royal trumpets, the crowd pressed forward excitedly. But when the emperor appeared, the crowd was shocked. The emperor was in his underwear!

Nobody in the crowd could see the emperor's suit, but of course no one would admit it out loud. Nobody wanted to look like a fool. Instead they offered praise.

"How handsome you look, your majesty. That certainly is a splendid suit," said one of the villagers.

"I never knew any fabric could look so wonderful," added another.

The king was delighted to hear such words of praise. Even though he couldn't see the fabric, he was now convinced there was no better in all the land.

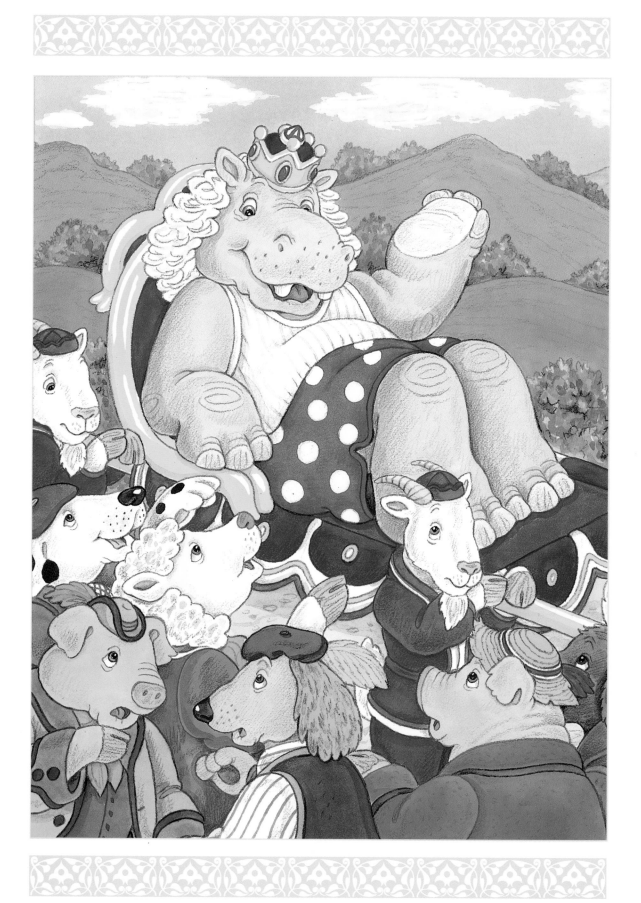

Suddenly a young boy cried out over the noisy crowd. "The emperor isn't wearing a new suit!" he said. "What is everybody talking about? The emperor is wearing nothing but his underwear!"

The emperor quickly turned to look at the crowd. They stood in stunned silence. Instantly the emperor knew the boy was telling the truth. He realized that he had been a fool, and now he was parading himself throughout the kingdom in his underwear.

All at once everyone in the crowd began to laugh. They had all been foolish, too. They pretended to see a suit that was not even there because they were afraid of what others would think.

After the parade, the embarrassed emperor quickly returned to the palace to put on some clothes. He ignored all his fancy and frilly clothes and chose to put on a simple blue robe with plain yellow buttons. "Ah, that's better." For the first time, the emperor left his room without looking in the mirror. Then he invited the honest young boy to speak with him in his court.

"I have decided to make you a junior minister," said the emperor. "You have shown that you are very brave because you told the truth when no one else would!"

The Little Mermaid

Adapted by Sarah Toast
Illustrated by Kathleen O'Malley

Deep, deep in the beautiful blue-green sea lived the sea king and his six mermaid daughters. Because the mermaids had fishtails instead of legs, they swam as easily and gracefully as the dolphins.

When each mermaid princess reached the age of fifteen, she was allowed to swim to the surface of the sea to view the ships and the towns on the far shore. Five of the mermaid sisters had already seen the surface. They told their younger sister, the littlest mermaid among them, about the strange creatures they had seen. The creatures were much like themselves, but they walked on land on two strange pegs called legs. The little mermaid begged her sisters to tell her all about the human creatures.

The littlest mermaid eagerly awaited the day when she would see the humans with her own eyes. Until that day came, however, she contented herself by playing with her sisters and swimming with her fish and dolphin friends.

To entertain herself, the little mermaid made up pretty songs to sing about everything that she enjoyed. She had such a lovely voice that all the creatures of the sea were drawn to its clear, pure sound. Even the sea king and his five other daughters loved to listen to the little mermaid's melodies.

At last the sea king said to his youngest daughter, "Your day has arrived. Today you may swim to the surface. Enjoy it, my daughter, but come back to us safely at the end of the day."

With a quick flash of her golden tail, the little mermaid swam upward. When she broke through the surface of the sea, she was thrilled to see a ship with many humans walking on the deck.

The little mermaid swam very close to the ship and saw a most handsome creature peering out at the horizon. "He has a golden crown on his head," said the little mermaid to herself. "He must be a prince!"

The little mermaid followed the prince's gaze and saw black thunderclouds moving in swiftly on the wind. Soon a terrible storm was raging. Thunder rumbled, and great, crackling flashes of lightning tore the sky in two. Huge waves tossed the ship.

As the little mermaid watched in horror, a bolt of lightning hit the great mast of the ship. The falling mast knocked several men overboard. Then the ship rose high on a wave, shuddered, and broke in two.

The little mermaid swam in among the splintered boards and barrels that crashed about in the waves. She swam frantically here and there looking for the prince.

At last she found him slipping down into the depths of the sea. The little mermaid had heard that humans cannot live long under water. With a flip of her golden tail, she whisked the prince to the surface, where he could breathe. Then the mermaid swam the long distance to the far shore, keeping the prince's handsome head out of the water. All the while she sang songs of hope and courage to him. Although the prince's eyes were closed, he heard the little mermaid's voice singing to him as if in a wonderful dream.

When at last they reached the shore, the little mermaid gently set down the prince on the sandy beach. She kissed his forehead softly, and quickly slipped back into the water to keep watch.

It wasn't long before a small group of humans found him. They recognized their prince immediately and made haste to the castle to get help. When the little mermaid saw that the prince was safe, she swam back to her father and sisters.

The sea king was concerned when his youngest daughter told him how much she loved a human. He was sad when the littlest mermaid told him how much she longed to be a human herself.

"I cannot help you, my daughter," said the sea king. "You are a mermaid, with the beautiful tail of a fish. We love you, and we are happy that you live here with us."

The little mermaid tried her best to be content, but every time she looked in the mirror, she saw a face that looked every bit like a human face. It set her to wondering why she couldn't be human. The little mermaid still sang her beautiful songs, but often now the words expressed her longing to be human so she could be with the prince.

When the little mermaid's friends heard her heartfelt songs, they felt sorry for her. At last a dolphin told her, "Sweet mermaid, there is a wicked sea witch who lives in a black cave in another part of the sea. It is said that those who get past her sea dragons and make their way into her cave sometimes get their wish."

"Dear friend," came the little mermaid's joyous reply, "I would brave any danger to become human so I can be with the prince."

"Brave mermaid," said the dolphin, "be careful. The sea witch will only help you if she can get something precious in return."

The little mermaid lost no time in swimming to the sea witch's cave. It was indeed difficult to get past the sea dragons, but the little mermaid was clever and swift. She burst into the sea witch's cave to find the witch gazing into a large glowing bubble.

"I know why you are here," said the sea witch in her raspy, gasping voice. "I see that you have saved a prince who fell into the sea. You fell in love with him. You want to be human."

"Yes, I do!" cried the mermaid.

"There is but one way to make you human, and that is to turn your fishtail into human legs. It will not be easy."

"What do you want from me in return?" asked the mermaid. In reply, the sea witch rasped, "You will have to give me the one thing that I want—your beautiful voice!"

The little mermaid thought of her love for the prince, and she agreed to the bargain. The sea witch gave her a magic potion.

"Swim quickly up to the surface," the sea witch instructed the little mermaid. "When you have reached the shore, drink this potion. You will have legs, and now—I have your voice!"

The sea witch's cackle turned into a lovely tinkle of laughter as the little mermaid swam away. As soon as she reached the sandy beach, the mermaid opened the bottle and drank its contents. In a blinding flash, she fell into a swoon.

A few minutes later the prince found the little mermaid on the sand. He often came this way to remember the beautiful voice of the gentle person who had saved him. Hoping he had found the woman with the lovely voice, the prince knelt down beside her.

Gently, the prince lifted the little mermaid's head and held her hand. The little mermaid awoke with her loved one's touch. Filled with happiness, she tried to speak. Her voice was gone completely.

When the prince did not hear the beautiful voice, he was very disappointed. Nevertheless, he was moved to help the lovely little maiden. He invited her to his castle.

Even though the little mermaid could communicate only with her hands and eyes, the prince was enchanted by her sweetness and beauty. The prince and the little mermaid saw each other every day. The little mermaid's human legs served her well for walking, for running along the sand as the waves lapped her pretty feet, and for her greatest new pleasure, dancing. Everyone said the little mermaid danced as light as sea foam and as gracefully as an angelfish.

The only thing that marred the little mermaid's happiness was that the prince did not love her. It was true that the prince enjoyed being with her, but he still longed to find the young woman with the beautiful voice who had saved him.

The little mermaid told herself every day that she must be glad to have gotten her wish to be human. She was grateful for her friendship with the prince and the pleasant days they spent together, even though he did not love her.

As much as the little mermaid enjoyed her life in the prince's castle, she often thought of her father and sisters under the sea. She thought fondly of her friends, the fish and dolphins.

The sea witch, meanwhile, consulted her glowing bubble to see how the little mermaid was faring. It gave her great satisfaction to know that the prince did not love her. But the sea witch had her own troubles. When she gave orders to her workers, they merely smiled and rippled in the currents. This was because the sea witch's voice was so lovely to hear. Even the glowing bubble quit showing the past and the future, and none of the sea witch's magic spells were working as well as before. The sea witch now realized that she needed her raspy, gasping voice back in order to do her evil magic.

"Little mermaid, little mermaid, I call you from the deep."

From far, far away, the little mermaid thought she heard her own voice calling her. She looked out toward the sea. Very far off, in the sea witch's part of the sea, she saw boiling black bubbles.

"Little mermaid, little mermaid, open your mouth and sing!" commanded her own voice from far out on the sea.

At her window the little mermaid did as the voice—her own voice—commanded. She opened her mouth and sang.

Suddenly the prince heard the beautiful singing. He looked out at the sea, remembering the voice of the young woman who had rescued him. This was her voice, he was certain!

The prince ran toward the enchanting voice. He stopped below the little mermaid's window, for there the voice was strongest. The prince looked up to see the little mermaid standing at the open window singing with pure love.

As soon as the little mermaid saw the prince, she ran to him. Breathlessly, she told him all that had happened. The prince thought that the little mermaid's voice was as beautiful in speech as it was in song. At last he knew he had found the young woman who had rescued him and sung to him, the woman of his dreams.

"Dear friend and loved one," said the prince, "I am sorry that I did not know who you were. All along, you were the one I was looking for. Please be my bride and live with me forever."

"Yes, I will," said the little mermaid. And they have been happy ever since.

The Selfish Giant

Adapted by Mary Rowitz
Illustrated by Sherry Neidigh

Every day after school several children played in the enchanted garden of a huge, empty castle. It was always summer in the enchanted garden. The trees never lost their leaves and the flowers always bloomed. Sometimes it rained in the garden, but only at nighttime when the children slept soundly in their beds.

In the enchanted garden the children skipped rope, swung from the tree branches, and played games. When they got hungry, they plucked fruit from the trees and ate it as they enjoyed the sunshine that never ended.

The children were happiest when they were in the garden. They loved to play there every day.

The empty castle did not stay empty for long. It belonged to a cruel giant who had been away for many years. One day he returned home hoping to find some peace and quiet after his long journey.

Instead he returned to the sound of laughter in his garden. He did not like what he saw when he looked over the garden wall. There were children playing all sorts of games and eating the fruit from his trees. This made the giant very angry. He wanted to have the garden all to himself.

"What are you children doing here?" the giant shouted. "This is my garden!" The giant did not want to share the beautiful things in his garden.

The giant's booming voice startled the children. They were so shaken that they could not answer his question. They didn't think to tell the giant how happy they felt when they played in the enchanted garden. But then the giant was in no mood to listen to reasons why he should share his garden.

He was a selfish giant.

The giant stormed into the garden and ordered all the children to leave at once. "Get down from those trees!" he roared. "Get out of my garden and never come back!"

The children didn't understand why the giant wanted them to leave. No one had ever sent them away before. Besides, the enchanted garden was big enough for everyone to enjoy. There was no reason the giant should keep it all to himself.

Still the children were scared of the grumpy giant. They ran from the garden as fast as they could. One little girl even forgot her jump rope.

Once the children were gone, the giant looked around the quiet garden and smiled. At last he was alone in his garden. But his smile disappeared when he saw the jump rope in the grass. "There will be no toys in my garden!" roared the giant, and he threw the jump rope over the garden wall.

"No noise, no toys, and no pesky children," muttered the giant to himself. "Just me and my garden." Finally he would have some peace and quiet.

He was a very selfish giant.

The children no longer had a place to play. They tried playing in other yards and gardens, but no place compared to their enchanted garden.

One day they stopped outside the garden wall. A curious boy wanted to see the garden with his own eyes, so he climbed onto a friend's shoulders and peeked over the garden wall. The boy gasped at what he saw. The leaves of trees were turning orange and falling to the ground. The grass was thin and brown. The flowers had wilted, and the birds had flown away.

"It looks like our wonderful garden is dying," said the child. All the children became sad. Their beautiful garden was no longer enchanted.

Soon the garden became a cold and lonely place. All the trees were bare, the grass was the color of straw, and the sun never shone there anymore.

One day the giant saw a flower poke its head through the ground. The giant watched the flower. He began to hope it would bloom. But then a strong gust of wind came and scared the flower back under the ground.

The giant didn't understand the changes that had taken place in his garden. When he returned from his journey, the garden was warm and full of life, but now it was dull and cold.

"At least now I have peace and quiet," the giant said, "and I don't have to share the garden with anyone."

The giant was simply being selfish.

The passing months brought even more changes to the garden. Snow blanketed the ground, icicles dangled from the walls of the castle, and cold winds ripped through the branches of the trees.

The giant now spent many hours watching the garden from a castle window. The giant could not figure out why it was so cold inside the walls of his garden. He knew that winter had ended, and the rest of the countryside was warm.

"Something is not right," the giant said. He began to wish for his beautiful garden and for the children who had made it such a happy place. For the first time the giant felt lonely.

By now the children had surely found another place to play, the giant thought. They no longer needed his garden to make them happy.

The giant was wrong. The children stopped outside the garden every day, wishing they could play there again.

One day, as a little child leaned against the garden wall, a stone wiggled loose and fell out.

"Look!" cried the child excitedly. "The stone has left a hole big enough to crawl through! We can all sneak into the garden. The giant will never know."

What a wonderful idea, thought the children. One by one they crawled through the secret passage. When their feet touched the ground, the snow in the garden began to melt. The grass turned green, and the sun began to shine again. When the children touched the trees, green leaves appeared. The birds came back and sang pretty songs. The children could not believe their eyes! They began to swing on the trees and jump in the grass. They were filled with joy to be back in the enchanted garden.

But in a small corner of the garden, icicles still hung from a single tree. A little boy looked up at the tree sadly. He wished he could climb the tree and swing on the branches. But he was too small to even reach the lowest branch.

The little boy anxiously circled the tree. He had waited such a long time to play in the trees in the enchanted garden. He could not give up now because he was too small. He sat down in the grass and tried to think of a plan.

Suddenly the boy felt a huge pair of hands gently lift him up and set him on one of the branches. This was certainly a good plan, thought the boy. Instantly the icicles that clung to the tree began to melt. Then tiny buds opened, and leaves sprouted all over the tree.

The surprised little boy turned to see the giant who had once roared with anger at the children. This time the giant did not roar. He seemed to welcome the little boy to the garden. The giant even smiled as he patted the little boy on the head.

The boy flung his arms around the giant's neck and kissed him on the cheek. The giant's heart melted as quickly as the ice and snow in his garden. He was sorry he had been so selfish.

At that very moment three buds poked their heads through the ground. The giant and the boy watched as they instantly bloomed into beautiful flowers.

When the other children saw that they no longer had to fear the giant, they rushed over to him. The giant scooped them up one by one and hugged them gently.

"Does this mean that we may play in your enchanted garden?" asked one shy child. The other children quietly waited to hear what the giant would say.

The giant now realized that it was the children who brought the magic to his garden. "From now on this is your garden," the giant said to the children. "You may come here to play whenever you wish. You can laugh here, run through the grass, and even play with your toys!" The children were delighted. The giant was no longer selfish.

All around them the enchanted garden was more beautiful than ever. The flowers and trees seemed to sparkle in the bright, warm sunshine.

The enchanted garden was more fun than ever, too. The giant became the children's favorite playmate. The children loved every minute they spent in the garden. And so did the giant—he had the most enchanted time of all.

The Fisherman and His Wife

Adapted by Sarah Toast
Illustrated by Rusty Fletcher

Once upon a time a poor fisherman and his wife lived in a little cottage near a river. Every day the fisherman went to the river and fished for their dinner.

One day the fisherman caught a magical fish in his net. It said, "Fisherman, I beg you to let me live. I am not really a fish, I am an enchanted prince. Please let me swim away."

The fisherman quickly agreed to let the fish go. "Say no more," said the fisherman. "I'm quite willing to set free a fish that can talk."

"For that, I'll grant you a wish," said the fish, but the fisherman said there was nothing he needed.

The fisherman let the fish go free. He fished in the river for the rest of the day, but he did not catch any fish. When he went home, his wife asked, "Husband, what have you caught for me to cook for our dinner?"

"I haven't brought anything home," he said. "I did catch a big fish. But he claimed to be an enchanted prince, so I threw him back into the water."

"Oh dear!" she said. "You might at least have made a wish before you set him free."

"I couldn't think of anything that we wanted or needed," replied her husband. The fisherman looked around his home. He was very satisfied with their little cottage. "What would you have wished for?" he asked his wife.

"Well, we certainly could use a nicer place to live. Why should we be satisfied with just a little cottage. I'm sure that if you go back to the stream and ask the fish for a nicer house, he will give it to you."

The fisherman did not really think that they needed a nicer house, but he did as his wife asked.

The fisherman returned to the river. He went to the same spot where he had caught the talking fish and called:

Princely fish that I set free,

Hear my words and come to me.

Just as soon as the fisherman had finished reciting this rhyme, the fish appeared. It held its head high above the water and looked directly at the fisherman.

"Why did you call me?" the fish asked.

The fisherman was a little nervous, but he got up his nerve. "My wife would like to make a wish after all," he answered. The fisherman anxiously waited for the fish's reply.

"And what is her wish?" asked the fish.

"She doesn't want to live in a tiny cottage anymore," said the fisherman. "She would like to live in a nicer home. I hope this isn't too much to ask of you."

"Go home to your wife," said the fish. "You will see that she already has her wish."

The fisherman hurried back home. There was his wife waving from the doorway of a pretty, new house.

The house was filled with everything they could possibly need. There was furniture in each room, and the cupboards were full of food. There was even a fireplace with a warm, glowing fire. "Now we can be happy," said the fisherman.

But a few days later his wife said, "Husband, this house is too small. We need more space. Go back to the river and ask the fish for a castle."

The fisherman wanted his wife to be happy, so he went back to the river and called:

> *Princely fish that I set free,*
>
> *Hear my words and come to me.*

Again, just as soon as the fisherman finished speaking, the fish appeared. "Now what?" asked the fish.

The fisherman thought the fish sounded a tiny bit angry. "Alas, I must ask another favor of you," the fisherman said regretfully. He nervously looked at the fish. "It seems as though my wife now wants to live in a castle."

"Go home. She is already there," said the fish. That said, the fish dove back into the river.

When the fisherman returned home, his wife waved to him from the balcony of a huge castle. Its rooms were full of golden furniture, and the tables were overflowing with wonderful things to eat.

"Isn't everything beautiful?" asked the wife. The fisherman nodded his head in agreement. He looked at all the things inside the magnificent castle. The fisherman thought that now they must have everything they could ever possibly want.

But early the next morning the wife woke up frowning. She said, "Husband, we live in a castle. It is only right that we should be king and queen of all the land."

The fisherman really didn't want to be king, but his wife insisted. The unhappy fisherman finally gave in and went back to the river. Once again the fisherman approached the spot where he had met the enchanted fish. And once again he called out:

> *Princely fish that I set free,*
>
> *Hear my words and come to me.*

The fish appeared as before. This time, though, the river and the sky seemed to get darker.

"What is it now?" asked the fish.

The fisherman was sure the fish was unhappy, but he asked his favor anyway. "I'm afraid my wife wants us to be king and queen," sighed the fisherman.

"Go home. She is already queen," said the fish.

Sure enough, when the fisherman arrived back at the castle, his wife was sitting on a golden throne. "Now that you are queen," said the fisherman, "surely you will not wish for anything more."

"I'm not at all sure of that," said the queen. "I have a feeling there is something else we need."

That night the fisherman slept well. His wife, however, lay awake tossing and turning. She was busy wondering what her next wish would be.

Just as the wife was about to fall asleep, the morning sun came up. Bright sunlight poured in through the bedroom window. The wife sat up in bed. How dare the sun shine through the royal window without her permission!

"Husband!" she called out. "Wake up at once. I have another wish to make!"

The husband rubbed his sleepy eyes.

"I do not think the sun should be allowed to rise without my permission. You go tell that enchanted fish of yours that I want to have complete power over the rising and setting of the sun," the wife demanded.

"Wife," said the fisherman, "please don't make me go back and call the fish again. I fear that this time the favor is too much to ask."

At this, the wife flew into a rage. "Go tell the fish to grant my wish!" she shouted.

Quaking with fear, the fisherman got dressed. He hurried out of the castle and headed toward the river. As he walked, strong winds began to blow, and the river began to rage.

The fisherman stumbled to the riverbank. The wind was so strong that he could barely hear his own voice. As he stood facing out over the water he called:

> *Princely fish that I set free,*
>
> *Hear my words and come to me.*

A bolt of lightning struck the ground, and a clap of thunder rang through the air. The fish rose up through the choppy waves.

"What does your wife want now?" bellowed the fish.

"Oh fish," said the fisherman fearfully, "she wants the power to make the sun rise and set."

"Go home to your wife," said the fish.

Suddenly the wind stopped blowing just as quickly as it had started. The waves in the river calmed, and the water was peaceful again. The fisherman went home. There stood his wife in front of their humble cottage. The great castle and all its golden furniture were gone.

"Husband," said the wife, "I am so sorry that I got carried away with greed. Each new and better thing only made me think I wanted more. But the more I got, the more unhappy I became. I forgot to be happy with what I already had."

"It's my fault, too," the fisherman said. "When you wanted more, I asked the fish for it."

The fisherman lovingly kissed his wife, took his net, and went to the river. He gazed into the clear blue water as he fished.

That night he returned to his cottage with a nice, plain fish for their dinner.

Goldilocks and the Three Bears

Adapted by Jane Jerrard
Illustrated by Burgandy Nilles

Once upon a time there was a bear family that lived in a lovely little house in the woods. There was great big Papa Bear, middle-size Mama Bear, and their baby, wee little Baby Bear.

They each had the right size chair to sit in: a great big chair for Papa Bear, a middle-size chair for Mama Bear, and a wee little chair for Baby Bear. And they each had a nice bed to sleep in that was just the right size.

Every morning for breakfast they ate a steaming bowl of porridge: a great big bowl for Papa Bear, a middle-size bowl for Mama Bear, and a wee little bowl for Baby Bear.

One fine morning Mama Bear made the family porridge while Papa Bear made up the beds. Mama Bear scooped the hot porridge into the three bowls: the great big bowl, the middle-size bowl, and the wee little bowl. Baby Bear licked his chops and spooned up a steaming spoonful of porridge, but Mama Bear stopped him before he could eat it.

"Wait, Baby Bear," said Mama Bear after she had tested her own porridge. "This porridge is much too hot to eat. It needs some time to cool."

The three bears decided to go for a walk while their porridge cooled. Mama Bear took her basket so she could gather sweet blackberries to stir into the porridge. Papa Bear put on his finest walking coat. Baby Bear carried his butterfly net. He loved to catch colorful butterflies in the woods and bring them home to live in his yard.

The three bears did not lock their door when they went out, because they were very trusting bears. They lived deep in the forest where they almost never had any visitors. They never expected anyone to enter their house while they were gone.

While the three bears were out walking, a little girl named Goldilocks passed by their lovely little house in the forest. Goldilocks had been out walking since early in the morning. She had not eaten any breakfast, and the three bears' porridge smelled very good to her.

Goldilocks looked in the window and saw the bowls of hot porridge sitting on the table. Goldilocks could hear her stomach rumbling with hunger. "That porridge looks delicious, and I am so hungry," said Goldilocks. "I'm sure no one will mind if I have a few bites."

Goldilocks slowly opened the door and went carefully into the lovely little house. She tiptoed through the kitchen. It was very quiet. All she could hear was the sound of birds singing outside. There was no one at home.

Looking around, Goldilocks saw many curious things. She saw three sets of slippers laid out for the next morning. One pair of slippers was for someone with great big feet. Another pair was for someone with middle-size feet. And the last pair was for someone with wee little feet.

Goldilocks looked and saw three jars of honey. Every jar was a different size, too. The whole house, Goldilocks noticed, was filled with three of just about everything in three different sizes! One was a great big thing, another was a middle-size thing, and the third was always a wee little thing.

This house must belong to a lovely little family of three, Goldilocks guessed. She thought they would not mind if she helped herself to just a little bit of porridge from one of the bowls on the table.

Goldilocks went right over to the table to taste the porridge. First she sampled the porridge in the great big bowl. "Ouch!" said Goldilocks, when the porridge burned her tongue. "This porridge is too hot!"

Then Goldilocks tasted the porridge in the middle-size bowl. "Oh no," she said. "This porridge is too cold."

Then Goldilocks tasted the porridge in the wee little bowl. She was too busy eating the porridge to say anything because it was just right. It was so good she ate it all up, and then she was sorry that the bowl did not hold more.

When Goldilocks finished the porridge, she decided to explore the little house. She wandered into the living room, where she found three chairs. Next to the great big chair was Papa Bear's jar of honey. In the middle-size chair was Mama Bear's colorful pillow. Behind the wee little chair was a whole shelf of books for Baby Bear to read.

Goldilocks was a little tired from her long walk through the woods, so she decided no one would mind if she sat down for a little while.

First Goldilocks sat in Papa Bear's great big chair. "This chair is much too hard!" she said. Next she sat in Mama Bear's middle-size chair. "This chair is much too soft," complained Goldilocks. Finally she sat in Baby Bear's wee little chair. "This chair is just right," said Goldilocks with a smile.

Goldilocks sat in the wee little chair, enjoying the peace and quiet. She was about to reach for one of Baby Bear's books when suddenly the little chair broke all to pieces. Goldilocks picked herself up off the floor and put the pieces back together as best she could. Then she decided to keep exploring.

Goldilocks went through the living room and found a little staircase leading upstairs. She tiptoed up the stairs and into the bedroom. Suddenly Goldilocks realized she was a little bit sleepy. "I've had such a busy day," she yawned. "I'm sure no one will mind if I just take a little nap."

First she lay down on Papa Bear's great big bed. "This bed is much too hard," said Goldilocks. Then she lay down on Mama Bear's middle-size bed. "This bed is much too soft," she said.

Goldilocks walked sleepily over to Baby Bear's wee little bed and lay down on it. "This bed is just right," said Goldilocks with a sleepy sigh. She snuggled under the covers and in no time was fast asleep.

By now the three bears thought that their porridge would be cool enough to eat, so they returned home. When they reached their little house, Baby Bear set his new butterflies free in the yard. Just then Papa Bear noticed that the front door of their house was open.

"This is strange," thought Papa Bear. "I'm sure I closed the door when we left this morning."

The three bears entered the house. Papa Bear looked around to see if someone had come to visit, but he didn't see anyone. "Maybe I forgot to close the door after all," he thought to himself.

The three bears were hungry after their walk and excited to have their breakfast. Papa Bear hung up his jacket, Baby Bear put away his butterfly net, and Mama Bear carried in her basket of berries. Then they all went into the kitchen.

The three bears sat down at the table and were about to eat their breakfast when suddenly they stopped. Something was not quite right.

Goldilocks had left the spoon standing in Papa Bear's bowl. "Someone has been tasting my porridge," Papa Bear growled in his great big voice.

Goldilocks had also left the spoon in Mama Bear's bowl. "Someone has been tasting my porridge," Mama Bear said in her middle-size voice.

Then Baby Bear noticed that his bowl was empty. "Look! Someone has been tasting my porridge and has eaten it all up!" he cried in his wee little voice.

Now the three bears knew that someone had been inside their house. They wondered if that someone was still there. The three bears went into the living room to look around. Something was not quite right. The three bears inspected their chairs.

Papa Bear walked up to his great big chair and saw that the cushion was a little crooked. He frowned and said in his great big voice, "Someone has been sitting in my chair."

Mama Bear saw that her colorful pillow was out of place. She frowned and said in her middle-size voice, "Someone has been sitting in my chair."

Then Baby Bear took a look at his wee little chair and cried in his wee little voice, "Someone has been sitting in my chair and has broken it all to pieces!" Baby Bear cried and cried about his broken chair. Mama Bear tried to fix it, but the pieces wouldn't properly fit back together.

Papa Bear looked around the room, trying to find their visitor. "Maybe our visitor went upstairs," said Papa Bear in his great big voice. With that, he climbed the staircase. Mama Bear followed. Baby Bear sniffled and followed along, too.

The three bears crept quietly into their bedroom. Just as in the kitchen and living room, something was not quite right. The bears looked closely at their beds.

Papa Bear noticed right away that his bedcovers were rumpled. "Someone has been sleeping in my bed," he growled in his great big voice.

Mama Bear saw that her pillows and quilts were a mess. "Someone has been sleeping in my bed," she said in her middle-size voice.

While Mama Bear and Papa Bear were busy looking at their beds and scratching their great furry heads, Baby Bear tiptoed over to his wee little bed. His eyes grew wide at what he saw there. Then he cried out in his wee little voice, "Someone has been sleeping in my bed, and there she is!"

Goldilocks awoke with a start. She saw the three bears standing beside the bed. Tumbling out of bed, she ran from the room. Down the stairs she went, as fast as she could.

The three bears never saw Goldilocks again, and that was just fine with them.

The Honest Woodcutter

Adapted by Jennifer Boudart
Illustrated by Tammie Speer Lyon

There once was a woodcutter who lived with his wife and two children in a forest far from town. Their house was not big or fancy, but it was warm and dry. The family was not rich, but they were happy and lived comfortably.

One morning the family joked about what their lives would be like if they had lots of money. The woodcutter wished for a bigger house, his wife dreamed of eating from fine china plates, and the children imagined playing with all sorts of wonderful toys.

When breakfast ended, the woodcutter put on his hat, grabbed his ax, and headed to work. His family stood on the porch of the house and waved good-bye to him as he walked deep into the forest.

The woodcutter worked in the oldest part of the forest, where the trees grew tallest and thickest. These trees were the hardest to chop down, but they were no problem for the woodcutter. He was very strong. The woodcutter simply sharpened his trusty old ax and went to work.

Soon wood chips flew through the air, and the forest echoed with the loud sound of the woodcutter's chopping. Although the woodcutter's ax was old, it suited him just fine. He took good care of it, and never considered getting a new one. He preferred to get new things for his family instead.

A little squirrel happened to be nearby collecting nuts, and she heard the noise of the woodcutter's ax. The squirrel went to see who was making all the noise.

"You are the fastest woodcutter I have ever seen!" said the amazed squirrel. She sat on a large pile of neatly stacked logs that the woodcutter had chopped earlier that morning.

The woodcutter did not notice the squirrel at all. He thought only about cutting more wood so he could give his family all the things they wanted.

Each day the woodcutter worked until noon and then took a short break. He liked to walk to the edge of the river to catch his breath. There he ate the lunch that his wife had prepared for him, and had a nice refreshing drink of water. The woodcutter never took too much time for lunch.

"I have to get back to work," he said to himself. "The more I work, the more wood I cut. And the more wood I cut, the better off my family will be."

This day, just like every other day, the woodcutter took his lunchtime break. He was very thirsty and walked quickly to the river to get a drink. All the while he was thinking about ways to make his family happy. If he had been paying more attention to where he was going, the woodcutter would have noticed a rock that was right in his path.

"Yikes!" shouted the woodcutter as he tripped over the rock. When he fell, the woodcutter's ax slipped out of his hands and landed in the middle of the river.

"Oh, no!" yelled the woodcutter. "I must get my ax back!"

The woodcutter picked himself up and ran to the edge of the water. He looked into the river, hoping to see his ax, but it was no use. The river was fast and deep. The ax was probably long gone by now.

The woodcutter was terribly sad. Without his ax, he could not chop wood. And without wood, he could not buy the things his family wanted. Without his ax, the woodcutter wouldn't even be able to buy food.

The woodcutter sat down on a nearby log. He hung his head and began to moan, "What am I going to do? That was my only ax! How can I earn a living for my family now?" He gazed sadly at the river's rushing water.

Suddenly the river started to make noise. The woodcutter looked up and saw the water rising. Then the water grew arms and a head, and it started to talk to him! "I am the water sprite, a fairy of this river. Why are you so sad?"

After the woodcutter told him what had happened, the water sprite said, "Don't worry. I can help you."

"I'll go down to the bottom of the river to find your ax," said the water sprite. In an instant the sprite was gone, and the river began to swirl and foam.

The woodcutter could not believe it! He would get his ax back and be able to help his family! After a few moments, the water sprite appeared again. This time the sprite held something in his watery hands. "Is this your ax?" he asked the woodcutter. "I found it in the rocks."

The woodcutter looked closely at the ax. He had never seen anything so magnificent. The ax was so shiny and beautiful. It was made of pure silver. Whoever owned it was rich indeed.

The woodcutter thought about taking the silver ax. He could sell it and buy many fine things for his family. There was just one problem, though. The ax did not belong to him, and it would be wrong to say it was his. Finally the woodcutter said, "I cannot take this ax. It is not mine."

The water sprite was surprised. He tossed the silver ax on the ground and said, "Very well, I'll look for your ax again."

Once again the sprite left to look for the woodcutter's ax at the bottom of the rushing river. And once again the river began to swirl and foam.

The woodcutter was hopeful that his ax would be returned to him. He watched the water anxiously. "I hope he finds my trusty old ax," he said to himself.

When the water sprite returned a few moments later, he held an ax that was more magnificent than the first one. It was made of solid gold. "This must be yours," said the sprite.

The woodcutter held the amazing gold ax for a moment. This ax could make him very rich. He could buy a big house in town, fine china dishes for his wife, and all the toys that his children could dream of. But the woodcutter gave the ax back to the sprite. "This is a fine ax, and you are kind to offer it to me," he explained. "But this ax is not mine. I am sure someone is looking for it and misses it."

The water sprite smiled and said, "Well, I see that you will take only your own ax. Let me look for it once more."

For a third time the magic water sprite left to look for the woodcutter's ax. When the sprite returned, he held another ax. This one was very different from the first two that he had offered the woodcutter. This ax wasn't shiny at all, and the handle was worn from use. The woodcutter smiled and said, "Ah yes! This is my ax."

The water sprite shook his head. "Are you sure you want this ax? The other two are so much finer."

"Yes, but they are not mine," said the woodcutter. He held his steel ax and said, "This ax has cut more trees than I can count. It was good enough for me before, so it must be good enough for me now."

The water sprite smiled and said, "Your ax is not worth much, but your honesty is. The silver and gold axes belong to me. I want you to take them as a gift for telling the truth."

The woodcutter couldn't believe his good fortune. He thanked the water sprite and decided to leave the forest early that day. Instead of going home, he went into the town to go shopping.

The woodcutter couldn't wait to get to the store. He was sure he could sell the axes to the store owner. When the woodcutter arrived, he handed the fine axes to the store owner. The owner looked them over carefully and finally said, "These are the best axes that I have ever seen. I will gladly buy them from you."

The store owner was very generous. He gave the woodcutter a large sack of gold coins. Now the woodcutter was rich! He bought an armful of beautiful flowers and a set of fine china plates for his wife. He also bought a big bag of toys for his children.

The woodcutter had lots of gold left over, and he carried it all back home with him. His wife and children jumped for joy when they saw the presents.

The woodcutter told his family all that had happened to him during the day. His son looked up at him and asked, "Why did the water sprite give you all three axes?"

Then the woodcutter's daughter said, "Because you told the truth, right?"

"That's right," said the woodcutter, "because I told the truth."

Puss in Boots

Adapted by Jane Jerrard
Illustrated by Susan Spellman

Once there was a poor miller who had three sons and very little else. When the old miller died, he left his mill to the oldest son and his donkey to the middle son. Because he had little else to give, he left his cat, Puss, to the youngest son.

The youngest son was upset over his poor share. "My older brothers can work together to earn a living," he said, "but Puss and I will surely die of hunger."

The cat overheard the boy. "Don't worry," said Puss. "Just give me a sack and a good pair of boots, and you'll see that I can be a great help to you."

"What good are boots and a sack for a cat with a poor owner?" sighed the boy. But he could do nothing else, so the boy did what the cat asked. He found an old grain sack by the side of the mill and a worn pair of boots in the rubbish pile.

When Puss got his boots, he dusted them off and pulled them on. He proudly strutted around the yard for a moment. Then Puss slung his new sack over his shoulder and walked to the edge of the woods, where many rabbits lived.

Puss picked some tender grass and fresh thistles and put them in the sack. Then he put the sack on the ground. He lay down next to it and pretended to be dead.

A plump, young rabbit soon hopped along and smelled the fresh thistles. The rabbit knew nothing about trappers, but he knew a lot about thistles. They were his favorite thing to eat. He crawled into the bag to have a quick snack.

Up jumped Puss. He grabbed the bag with the rabbit inside and slung it over his shoulder. Puss marched through the woods and went straight to the royal palace, where he knocked on the big front door and asked to see the king.

Puss was led into the king's throne room. He made a low bow before the king and said, "Sire, I bring you this gift from my kind master, the Duke of Carabas." The king was a good king, but he was not known as a very smart king. He couldn't quite remember a Duke of Carabas, but he thought the name sounded very important.

Puss, on the other hand, was very smart. The king didn't know that Puss had just made up the title for the miller's youngest son, who was not a duke at all.

Nevertheless, the king was very pleased to have a delicious rabbit for his dinner. "Tell your master," the king said to Puss, "that I thank him and accept his gift with pleasure."

The next day Puss caught two plump partridges and again went to the castle to present them to the king. The king was pleased and said, "Thank your generous master, the Duke of Carabas. He is most kind."

Every day for many weeks, Puss brought a different gift to the king. The curious king began to wonder about this mysterious Duke of Carabas.

One day Puss found out that the king was taking his beautiful daughter for a drive along the river. Suddenly he came up with an idea. Puss said to his master, "Go down to the river, take off your shirt and trousers, and jump in. Leave the rest to me."

The boy did not understand why Puss asked him to do this. "I don't see what good this will do," he grumbled. "I found a sack and boots for you, but as far as I can tell, no good has come of it. We are still poor." But in his heart the boy trusted Puss. He left his shirt and trousers on the riverbank and jumped into the water. Then Puss hid his master's clothes under a big stone.

Before long they heard the king's coach come rumbling down the road. Puss ran in front of the coach and cried out, "Help! Help! My master, the Duke of Carabas, is drowning in the river!"

The king stopped the coach when he saw Puss. "The Duke of Carabas?" thought the king. "Why, he is the kind gentleman who has provided me with so many delicious feasts." He ordered his guards to rescue the duke. The princess peeked out the window of the coach and watched the guards pull the boy from the river.

Puss went up to the coach and poked his head inside the window. He smiled at the beautiful princess, who looked very concerned for the boy. Then Puss told the king that robbers had stolen his master's clothes and thrown him into the river where he was left to drown.

The king wanted to help. He ordered one of his guards to ride quickly back to the palace and bring the unfortunate duke a dry, warm set of clothes.

The boy could not believe his luck when the king's guard arrived with a fine suit of clothes for him. Dressed in his new garb, the boy did indeed look like a duke. He went to the coach to thank the king for his help.

The princess certainly thought the boy looked handsome. The boy certainly thought the princess was beautiful. When the Duke of Carabas glanced at her shyly, the princess smiled back sweetly. The king saw the attraction between the two young people and smiled. Then he asked the young duke to ride with them. Although he was not a smart king, he certainly knew how to make his daughter happy.

Puss, meanwhile, went ahead of the royal carriage to carry out his plan. He spoke to several farmhands who were hard at work cutting hay in a field. "When the king comes along, you must tell him that this field belongs to the Duke of Carabas. If you don't, the ogre who lives in the castle on the hill will chop you into tiny pieces!" Puss glared at them.

Sure enough, when the king drove up, he asked the farmhands who owned the land they were working. They answered, "The Duke of Carabas!"

The king thought the farmhands looked a little nervous. "Perhaps they have never spoken to a king before," he thought to himself.

A little farther down the road, when the king asked another group of farmhands who owned the land they were working, they also said, "The Duke of Carabas!"

"These farmhands are a bit nervous as well," thought the king. "Their master the Duke of Carabas must be a very powerful man. Or they have never spoken to a king before."

And so it went. Puss sat on a hilltop nearby, watching the king's progress. He was very pleased with his plan so far.

Everywhere the king asked, he was told that the land belonged to the Duke of Carabas. The king was amazed at how much land the duke owned and how many workers he had.

"This Duke of Carabas must be very wealthy indeed," thought the king. "Not to mention loyal and generous, for he has provided me with many a fine feast."

But while the king was admiring the duke's many lands, the princess was not paying attention to his wealth at all. She made sure he had not caught a chill from his swim in the river. She gazed into his eyes and talked with him throughout the entire journey. The duke was the most kind and handsome man the princess had ever met.

The duke, in turn, thought the princess was truly the most beautiful and wonderful woman he had ever met. He pulled down the shade on the carriage window so that her eyes would not catch the glare of the sun. He rearranged the pillows in the carriage so that she would be more comfortable. By the time they approached the royal palace, the princess felt she loved the duke. And the duke was sure he loved the princess.

While the princess and the duke talked and got to know one
another, Puss ran ahead to the ogre's castle. The ogre was the true
owner of the land. His many workers were very afraid of him.

The ogre was very rich indeed. In addition to his land, he had
heaps upon heaps of treasure hidden away in his castle. He spent
most of his days sitting in his castle, counting his gold and admiring
his treasures.

The horrible ogre was also said to have special powers. Puss
had heard that he could change himself into any animal he chose.
Puss had a plan to see the ogre's magic for himself.

When he arrived at the castle, Puss demanded to see the ogre.
Puss was ushered into the throne room, where the huge ogre sat
on a tiny velvet stool.

Puss said to him boldly, "I have heard of your great powers to
change yourself into any animal you choose, even a lion or an
elephant!"

"It is true," roared the ogre, as he changed into the form of a
fearsome lion. Puss leaped up onto a cupboard. He jumped down
when the ogre turned himself back into an ogre.

Puss lied to the ogre and said that he was very frightened. Then he said, "I have heard that you can also change yourself into a tiny animal, even a mouse. But that's impossible!"

"What? Impossible?!" roared the ogre. "Not impossible for me!" In the blink of an eye, he changed himself into a little mouse. Puss wasted no time. He pounced on the mouse and gobbled it up. As the mouse was gone, so was the ogre.

Meanwhile the king's coach had arrived at the castle. Just as the king asked whose castle it was, Puss ran out to welcome the king and the princess. Puss said, "Welcome to the castle of the Duke of Carabas!"

"Don't tell me this fine castle is yours!" exclaimed the king.

The duke merely smiled and led the king and the princess into the great hall.

Together they enjoyed a splendid feast. Then the king offered the charming duke his lovely daughter's hand in marriage.

The duke and the princess were married that day. As for clever Puss, he lived a life of ease in his master's castle ever after.

THE
END

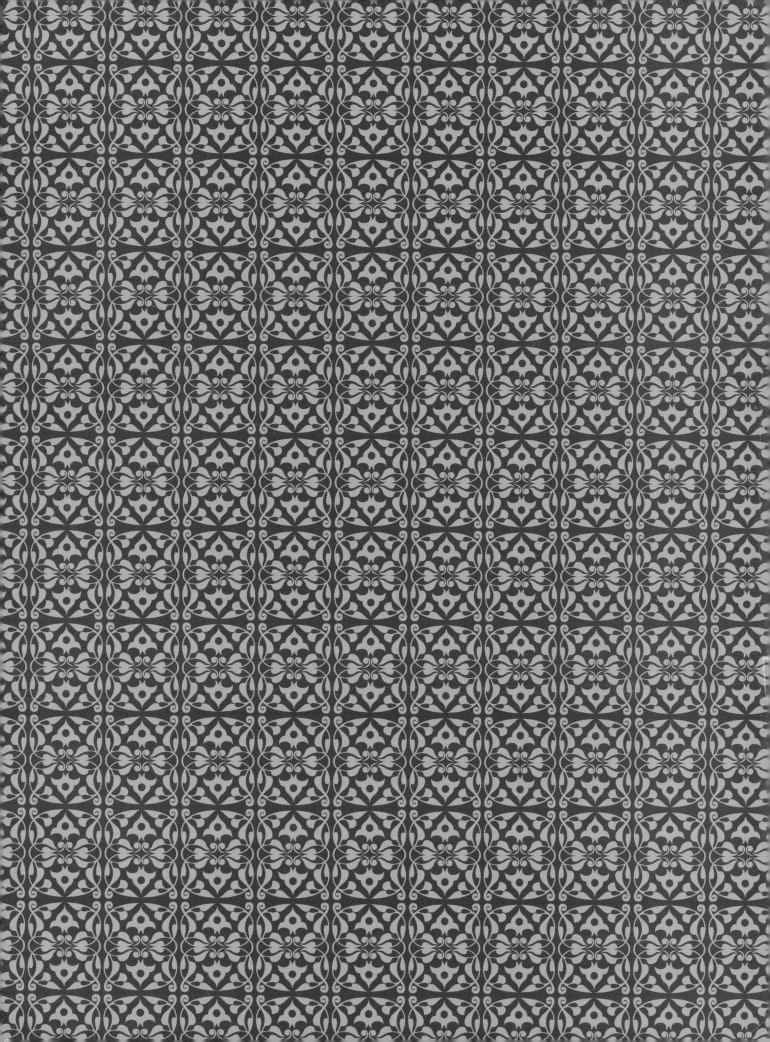